D1103454

JOSEPH LAMB

the

GOD

of all

SMALL

BOYS

pokey
hat

First published in 2019 by Pokey Hat

Pokey Hat is an imprint of Cranachan Publishing Limited

Copyright © Joseph Lamb 2019

The moral right of Joseph Lamb to be identified as the author of this work has been asserted by him in accordance with the Copyright, Designs and Patents Act, 1988.

All rights reserved.

No part of this publication may be reproduced, stored in a retrieval system or transmitted in any form or by any means, electronic, mechanical, photocopying, recording or otherwise, without prior permission of the publisher.

ISBN: 978-1-911279-40-2
eISBN: 978-1-911279-41-9

Interior Illustrations © Charlotte McIntosh

Cover Illustration: Boys Running in the Sun
© Jorgenmac | Dreamstime.com
Landscape, sunny dawn in a field
© shutterstock.com / Maxim Khytra

Lyric: The God of All Small Boys (song) by Dave Leigh, based on a manuscript by Joseph Lamb, 2014
(used by kind permission of Dave Leigh)

www.cranachanpublishing.co.uk

@cranachanbooks

PRAISE FOR
THE GOD OF ALL SMALL BOYS

'Beautifully written, refreshingly direct and clear—
meticulously researched; set in a rich and atmospheric world
that is solid yet haunting.'

Theresa Breslin
Carnegie Medal Winner

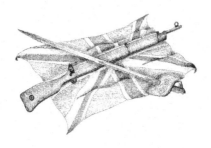

This book is dedicated to the memories of My
Grandparents:
Jim and Christina Gunning, Janet and Harold
Moir.
Also to the ever-lasting memories of my father
(Joe Lamb), my Uncle Les—and of my wee brother,
Kevin.

With much love to my mother, Mary, and to
my long-suffering and patient wife Ashleen—and
Murray and Finlay.

And ever, and always... *for Charlotte.*

1

AUGUST 1917

A slim ray of sunshine slanted through the slight gap in James's bedroom curtains, catching tiny dust motes that sparkled in the light. The clock in the parlour chimed, announcing to the Gunning household that it was half past eight. James barely noticed it. He sat by his dresser, still in his pyjamas, despite having been up and awake for at least an hour. The butterflies that crowded his belly left him unable to do anything, never mind sleep.

He glanced at the cedar chest at the foot of his bed. His school clothes lay on top of it, pressed, folded and lain out for him during the night. He sighed and turned back to the photograph he had been staring at.

His parents gazed out from their gold-edged frame. His father looked so young: serious-faced, dressed in an immaculate, kilted uniform, the photograph having been taken the day he had joined the Black Watch army.

James's mother stood by him: pretty, a little shy, almost smiling.

It was the only photo James had of her. He sighed and wished for the millionth time that she hadn't died.

A light tapping sounded from his bedroom door. It opened just a crack.

'Are ye up, Master James?' A familiar voice asked an equally familiar question.

'Yes, Toosh, I am.'

The housemaid bustled into the room and flung the curtains wide. Bright sunlight flooded in.

'Mmnnn... Too bright,' James grumbled. He wasn't keen on early mornings, and as much as he enjoyed going to school, he still wished the holidays had lasted a little longer. He and his father had actually managed to spend three days together during the holiday fortnight.

'Aye, well. Come and have yer breakfast. Busy day today, remember? The Captain's almost ready to go.'

'What!' James cried, his early-morning grumps forgotten. 'Already?'

He jumped up, knocking over the chair in his haste, and dashed downstairs to the sitting room. His father stood by the front door, wearing his full uniform, topped with a heavy overcoat. A large, brown valise and a dun-coloured kit bag sat at his feet.

James ran to him. 'Don't go, Daddy!'

'I'm sorry, James, but I must. My men need me.'

James's face turned cold. His vision blurred with tears as he clutched his father's arm. 'But so do I. Father, please!'

Mr Gunning dropped to one knee and James flung his arms around his father's neck. The young boy sobbed, his cries muffled by the overcoat's thick collar.

The tall man let his son hold him for a moment. Then he took James gently by the shoulders and moved him back. The boy dropped his head, ashamed of his tears.

'Look at me, son.'

James wiped the sleeve of his pyjama jacket across his face and lifted his head. His eyes were drawn to the bright, red-feathered hackle pinned to the side of his father's Glengarry cap. The fluffy badge seemed to shimmer as Mr Gunning spoke of his duty.

'I told you that, once I trained my men, I would be leaving for France, yes?'

James nodded.

'Well, that time has come. My men are ready, and I must join them. We will do our best to make the King and country proud, and make the German armies wish they had never heard of the Black Watch.'

James bit at his bottom lip. He had been dreading this day. His father's departure meant he would have to leave his home, his school, and all of his friends. His gaze flickered to Mary and Christine. The housekeepers' eyes were crinkled and red-rimmed, their lips drawn in tight lines, as they came to stand beside him.

'Do you understand, James?'

James blinked. He hadn't heard his father's last words, but he gave a little nod and mumbled a quiet "*yes*" under his breath.

His father gave a tiny smile. 'And what do we say?'

'On the ba', Dundee!' James tried to smile back.

His father stood straight and adjusted his cap by the smallest amount. 'Good. So, no school today, and Christine will take you there this afternoon.'

But I don't know where I'm going! James thought. *What did he just say?*

He had missed something important but didn't trust his voice to be able to speak, without breaking into sobs.

'Very well, my little soldier, march to your room. I shall write as soon as I am able and will see you when I return. I am sure the war will be all over by Christmas!'

His father spoke in his *Captain's Voice*. Whenever James heard it, he imagined his father drilling his soldiers: barking out orders to the kilted troops, and the men obeying his every word.

Mr Gunning snapped to attention and threw his son a smart salute. James clumsily returned the gesture then turned to hug Mary, fearing he would weep again as his father lifted his bags. The housekeeper stroked James's hair and made small comforting noises.

The front door closed, its latch snapped like a gunshot,

and James tore out of Mary's arms. He ran to the door, threw it wide and darted outside, but had only taken a few steps before he slammed to a halt. His slippered feet skidded, throwing gravel in every direction, as he stared—slack-jawed and wide eyed—at the gleaming, black automobile which sat on the driveway.

Motor cars were not a novelty to James. He often saw them driving along the beach road, heading towards Broughty Castle and the East Sands. But this vehicle was no rattling runabout. Every inch of it glimmered in black and steel. Its engine thrummed. Even the rubber of its running boards reflected the sun, as bright as the silvery statue which sat on its bonnet.

James stood transfixed, until the slam of the carriage door broke his trance. He jerked his head around to find his father settling himself inside the vehicle, as the driver returned to the front seat.

'Daddy!'

Unmindful of his pyjamas, James dashed to the carriage, his face streaked with fresh tears. Captain Gunning smiled gently and raised a hand in farewell, as the motor-car eased away, glinting and purring as it crunched over the gravel.

Every part of James urged him to chase after the car but, before he could move, Mary and Toosh came to stand at his side. Mary took his left hand, Toosh, his right, and all three watched as the car turned onto Cedar

Road and vanished from view.

'It'll be fine, Master James. Don't worry yourself none,' Mary's voice was soft and low.

'But why can't I just stay here?' James sniffed.

Mary and Toosh bent to envelop James in a hug, and he clung to them.

For most of his life, he had been raised by these two formidable housemaids. Mary, the elder of the two, was Irish-born, which was reflected in her blonde hair, deep green eyes and quick, cheery smile. The other, Christine— or *Toosh*, as James called her—was Dundonian to the bone; with thick, auburn hair and deep, dark eyes.

These women scolded him when he made too much noise, or left his hoop in the hallway, or tracked mud into the kitchen, where they sat and drank cup after cup of strong, black tea. They also ran James's baths, washed his clothes, dressed his scraped knees, and kissed him on the forehead every night when he went to bed. *What would he do without them?*

'You could look after me, couldn't you?' James asked, his eyes pleading.

The women shared a sorrowful look.

'It's just not the done thing, sweetheart,' Mary said. 'Not the done thing at all.'

James held the women's hands even tighter, as they stood in silence, watching the corner of Cedar Road, as if waiting for something they knew would never return.

2

LOCHEE

The River Tay glinted at James as he stared out of the window of the clattering tram. His forehead pressed against the cool glass while the coastline, the Railway Bridge, and the far hills of Fife, slid out of sight, to be replaced by buildings of flaking red-brick and grime-stained glass.

He slumped in his seat.

'Don't worry, Master James,' Toosh said. 'I bet you'll hardly have time to get settled before the Kaiser gives up, and we're all back home again.' She forced a smile, but James was not taken in by it.

The tram trundled on, and James caught sight of the Dundee Law, a massive hill, which rose at the centre of the city. Tantalising glimpses of it flashed between the buildings, until it too fell behind him.

Toosh shifted in her seat. She peered through the

window, as if searching for something, or someone, when the tram conductor called out.

'Lochee Depot! Everybody off!'

'This'll be us, then,' Toosh's voice wavered.

James grabbed at her hand and held tight, as the other passengers hurried by. The air was hazy with smoke and steam, and James spluttered as his breath caught in his throat.

Toosh rummaged in her coat pocket and pulled out a scrap of paper. 'Now, Master James...' she muttered 'If that's the High Street, then we need to go... this way!'

As they followed the noisy streets, James's eyes darted everywhere. Grey, soot-caked buildings rose from streets which were uncluttered, but looked terribly old. A cart or two sat at the roadside, and the vendors' voices overlapped as they cajoled the crowd of shoppers to buy oysters, fruit, or books.

James gasped, as a group of small children ran by, each one barefoot and their feet black with dirt.

'Here we are.' Toosh stopped outside a long building.

Dark entrances led into the depths of the wide tenement block. The tightness in James's stomach leapt to his throat, and he squeezed Toosh's hand as she entered one of the gloomy hallways. At the far end stood a worn, leaf-green door and a spiral flight of stone stairs.

Climbing the steps, they came around the curve to find the stairwell opened onto a wide, door-filled corridor.

'It's not this pletty, James, it's the next one up,' Toosh said, and continued to climb.

As they reached the next landing, James shaded his eyes against the sudden light and saw a row of windows and doors stretched out left and right. Behind him, a waist-high, metal railing ran the length of the building.

Toosh glanced at the piece of paper in her hand and studied the doors for a moment. 'It should be just down here a bit.' She marched along the corridor to a dark brown door and rapped her knuckles on the wood.

A minute passed. Toosh checked the paper, and lifted her hand to knock again, just as the door flew open.

'Aye? What? Who are you?' A young man with tousled hair peered at them. 'My mother's no' in... Oh!' His eyes opened wide. 'You must be... Jamie, is it?'

'It's James,' Toosh said. 'Are you Robert or John?'

The young man grimaced. 'How d'ye know who...? Och, aye, of course. I'm Robert. John's still at his work. In fact, so's Mum and Dad. Are ye no' a wee bit early?'

Toosh shrugged. 'Not as far as *I* know. The Captain said to be here by early afternoon, so here we are.'

James took a nervous step back, as Robert looked at him. 'Ahh, so you're my wee cousin, eh? Well, come away in.' He stepped back from the doorway.

Toosh hesitated for a moment, then led James into the darkened house.

'There's the kitchen,' Robert pointed to the left. 'The

bedrooms are on that side, and the living room's through here. It'll be a wee bit cauld, though. The fire's no lit yet.'

'So, your parents aren't home?' Toosh asked.

'No. Like I said, they're still at the mill. Mum'll be back soon-ish though.'

'Oh...'

'Have a wee seat anyway. It'll be some wait for ye. We've got some auld newspapers at the side o' the fire for kindling. Ye could have a look through them if ye want? Or would ye maybe like a wee cuppie?'

'Oh... No, no thank you. I've got a lot on this afternoon... I just... I thought Mr or Mrs Harkins would be here. Well, off you go and sit down, James. I'm sure I'll see...' Toosh's words stuck in her throat, as James threw his arms around her and sobbed.

'Oh, Master James! Please, don't cry. Everything'll be fine. I'll see you as soon as we can. You're with your family now. You've nothing to worry about. Remember, you're your dad's wee soldier!'

James snuffled and nodded.

Toosh's eyes glistened. 'Go and sit down, Master James. Robert can see me out.'

James stepped back to the fireside chair and fell into it. His head throbbed as he struggled to stop more tears from falling. But, as Robert led Toosh back to the front door, he gave up the fight.

3

BILLY MEETS JAMES

Billy Harkins raced up the tenement stairs, away from his mother, and barged through his front door, which opened with a loud crash.

He darted inside, ran to his bedroom and flung himself onto the bed. Then, burying his face in the blankets and pillows, he burst into tears. His hands throbbed, still painful from having been belted at school, just before the bell.

'Is that *you*, Billy?' His brother, Robert's, voice came from the kitchen.

'Aye,' Billy forced out, his voice cracking. 'I'm just having a lie down.'

As his sobs lessened, he heard the front door close, and his mother's voice drifted in from the hall. Billy tried to make sense of the muted buzz, but for some reason, she was speaking far more quietly than usual.

He slipped into sleep and began to dream of wandering his school corridors, peeking into darkened rooms. He was looking for *something*, but didn't know what.

Then the bedroom door flew open, shattering his dream.

'William Harkins! Get off o' that bed!' His mother's voice hammered into his pounding head.

Billy jolted up and swung his legs over the edge of the bed. He sat there for a moment, his head hanging forward. But his mother's voice gave him no mercy.

'I said, get UP!'

'I'm comin',' he slurred. He smacked his lips, his tongue thick and sticky in his mouth.

'Get intae the kitchen, it'll be tea-time soon.'

Nearly tea-time! How long was I asleep? Billy turned, but his mother was gone. He could hear her through in the kitchen—fussing around someone—but speaking in a voice that sounded… different.

Hang on! Why is she talking all posh? Curiosity cleared his head, and he sprang from the bed and ran through to the kitchen.

He stopped dead.

There—standing in the middle of the room—was another boy. Billy looked him up and down, his face a picture of disgust.

The stranger's shoes were spotless, made of shining black leather, and they were *real* shoes, not rough, ankle-high boots. He wore full-length trousers—not the shorts that Billy and his friends wore—which were a deep, sooty black.

'Billy, this is James.' His mother said, in that odd voice. 'He has come to stay with us for a wee while because his dad—your uncle—has gone over to France tae fight in the war.'

Billy tried not to smile, as his mother's *posh* voice faltered. To cover his laughter, he turned and looked at James. He had heard of his cousin—mostly when his mother used James as an example, to let Billy know how awful *he* was.

Whenever she caught Billy doing something he shouldn't have been doing, it was almost guaranteed that at some point during his dressing-down his mother would throw in a, *"ye widnae catch James Gunning doin' that!"*

The boy who stood before him wasn't what he'd imagined at all.

But still, Billy *hated* him on sight.

'Now, James,' Billy's mother spoke to the interloper. 'Ye've caught me a bit off guard. I wasn't expecting you until this evenin'. But we'll get ye settled tonight, then tomorrow we'll walk ye up tae school a wee bit early, and you can see somethin' o' Lochee. Does that sound good?'

'Yes, Mrs Harkins,' James said.

'Oh, dinnae be *Mrs Harkins*-ing me, James. That's

silly! I'm yer Auntie June!'

'Oh, sorry... Aunt June.'

'There ye are! Auntie June!' She beamed. 'Now, this is Billy, yer cousin.'

Billy glanced at James in a begrudged greeting.

'Dinnae mind him, James. He's still grumpy 'cos he got the belt just afore he got oot o' school.'

'Mu-uuum!' Billy protested, but his mother ignored him, still talking to the other boy.

'Anyway, James, yer Uncle Wullie, and John, and Alice, will be hame soon, so ye'll meet them later on. It'll be a wee bit cosy with all o' us in here, but I'm sure we'll be fine. You an' Billy can share the same end o' the bed.'

James's mouth dropped open, and Billy grinned at his cousin's look of horror.

Aye, you'll not be used to sharing a bed with three other laddies, will you? He thought.

The thin squeak of a motor horn drifted into the room, and Billy's face lit up, his annoyance forgotten. He ran into the living room to look out of the window.

In the gathering dusk, at the top of the hill, a small motorcar puttered along, followed by a throng of laughing boys and girls. The driver waved and chuckled along with the children, as he trundled slowly through Lochee.

'Look, Mum!' Billy's voice rose in excitement. 'It's a Ford!'

'Och, a motorcar's just a motorcar.' She shuffled into

the room, with James close behind her. 'They aw' look the same tae me.' She turned to her nephew. 'Ye'll have seen a motor or two in the Ferry, eh James?'

'Yes,' James said. 'A Rolls Royce came for my daddy this morning.'

Billy spun from the window.

'Liar!' he spat the word out. 'No-one in Dundee owns a Rolls Royce. They're too dear - they cost nearly five hundred pounds!'

James's face hardened into a stare of anger.

'I am NOT a liar! It came and took my father away. *It took my father away*!' James roared the last words at the top of his voice and took a step towards his cousin.

Billy was no stranger to a scuffle, and as James stepped forward, Billy stepped backwards, curling his hands into fists. But, before either could make another move, they were both dragged backwards by their collars.

Mrs Harkins shook them, jangling their bodies back and forth by the scruff of their necks. 'Hey! That's enough! I'm no' havin' the two o' ye fightin' like dogs in the street! William Harkins, get back in that bedroom. Now!' She pushed Billy away.

Billy gave James a glare, then stormed off to his bedroom and threw himself upon his bed once more.

TEA *AND* SYMPATHY

'James Gunning,' Mrs Harkins planted her hands on her hips. 'I'm surprised at ye, shoutin' like that! I'm black-affronted, so I am.'

'But… but it did, Auntie June. The Rolls Royce took my daddy away.' James flung his arms around his aunt and sobbed into her woollen cardigan.

His aunt hugged back, stroking his hair as he clung to her. 'Aw, there-there, James. It's all a bit much for ye, is it?'

James barely heard his aunt's question. The warmth of his breath made the coat give off a scent; a heavy, almost spicy aroma. That same odour lingered about Lochee. It was the smell of the mills—of the strange, fibrous jute and flax plants which were spun and twisted into threads, then woven into rough cloth and sacking. The dust from those fibres covered everything in the large

16

buildings: the looms, the rafters, the people and their clothes.

James stepped back and stared out of the window, watching the car as it carried on down the road. He marvelled at the children who danced alongside it. Their clothes were grubby and ragged, and at least two of them were barefoot. But it took a moment before James realised what was missing... There were no parents, no housekeepers! Not a *Mary* or a *Toosh* in sight. The children were just... playing—*alone*—in the streets!

His head reeled. *This is like a different world*!

'C'mon back intae the kitchen. We'll have a wee blether afore tea-time, eh?' said Aunt June.

James let himself be guided back to the kitchen table and stood there, with his shoulders hunched. A flame burned in the fireplace and a large copper kettle sat above it on a metal grill.

Robert came into the kitchen carrying a bulky paper sack.

'Crivvens, Mum, what's in this?'

'Tatties. Put it doon aside the cupboard, wid ye? And James, you hae a seat, it'll be a wee bit cosier in here now the fire's on. Robert should've got this going when he came in.'

'Aye, no problem, Mum! It's no' like I've been working, eh?' said Robert.

'Aye and it's no' as if *I've* no' been working as well, and a wee bit harder than you. Now take that cheek o' yours out o' my kitchen!'

Robert grinned. 'Dinnae worry, James. She's only like this all the time.'

He ducked and laughed as a rag sailed over his head. 'Ye missed, Mum! Yer gettin' tae be a bad shot in yer auld age.'

'I'll *auld age*, ye, ye cheeky besom!'

Robert dashed back into the bedroom.

'I tell ye, James, I hope ye're no' as cheeky as that wee get!' the woman said.

'Umm…' James began.

'Och, he's no' really that bad. But him and his brother are a right pair o' rascals. Now then, I've got the kettle on the fire, and we'll make ye a wee cuppie when it boils. Did Robert no' ask if ye wanted anything?'

James opened his mouth to reply, but never got the chance to speak.

'I widnae put it past him. Typical laddie. Disnae think o' anybody but himsel'. Just like his faither.'

The woman never stopped moving around the kitchen as she spoke. She fetched two cups from a shelf, and a small metal box from another. Flipping the box open, she spooned some tealeaves into a large, brown teapot. The kettle's lid began to rattle, and the woman wrapped a rag around its handle and poured the steaming water into the waiting teapot.

'We'll have tae give this a minute,' she said, then spun on her heel and swiped open a large purple curtain which hung at one end of the room.

Behind the drape, in a tight alcove, sat a double bed. James stared, baffled by the sight.

There's a bed in the kitchen?

The woman smoothed out the worn sheets which covered the bed, then returned to the teapot and poured out two cups of tea.

'Here ye go, James. Ye cannae beat a good cuppie tea, eh?'

James sipped at his hot, sweet tea and stared around the kitchen. It looked very old but it was quite clean. His eyes kept being drawn to the bed in the alcove. He had never seen such a thing, and he smiled, wondering what Mary and Toosh would have thought of it.

He was jolted from his thoughts as Aunt June spoke again.

'You needin' another cuppie?'

'Oh, no, I don't think so,' James whispered.

'Well, dinnae worry if ye ever do. We're all tea-hands here. The kettle's never off the fire!'

James tried to smile, but his aunt's face softened. She dragged another chair next to his and sat down.

'What's the matter wi' ye, son?'

James's eyes glistened in the firelight. 'I... I didn't want my father to go to war. I didn't want to leave my school.

I would've started Primary Six this week. And I miss David,' he whispered.

'Aw, is that one o' yer pals?'

James sniffed and wiped at his eyes. 'Yes, David Martin. He's my best friend. His father can't go to the war.'

'Aye, yer Uncle Wullie's the same. He's been tryin' tae join the Black Watch since this palaver started, but they'll no' let him in. He used tae be a whaler, y'see, but his leg got crushed during a catch, and he's got a bit o' a limp. He's too stubborn tae ask yer daddy tae help him, though.'

'Ask my daddy?'

'Aye, well, what with him being a Captain and all. I'll tell ye the truth James, if yer mammy was still alive, I'd have gotten *her* tae ask him, but, well...'

'My mother?'

'Aye, it's an awful shame.' Aunt June paused for a moment. 'D'ye know I offered tae take ye in when yer mammy died?'

James shook his head, speechless.

'Aye, but yer dad was havin' nane o' it, though. But now look,' she spread her arms wide, 'here ye are! Changed days, eh?'

His aunt smiled; her words came quickly, and James found them a bit difficult to understand. He fought against the crush of loneliness and forced a smile back at her.

5

TEA-TIME

'What's goin' on here then?'

James jumped in his seat and turned towards the kitchen door. A tall man stood there, filling the doorway.

'Oh this is wee James, is it?'

'Aye, it is,' said Aunt June. 'And where have *you* been Wullie Harkins?'

'Ach, me and Norrie Connel were…'

'It disnae matter. Is John wi' ye?'

'Aye,'

'Then sit doon, yer tea's nearly ready… TEATIME!'

Aunt June bellowed the last word towards the doorway. A rumble of footsteps was heard as the rest of the Harkins trooped into the room.

'Aye, there's one or two mair o' us than ye'll be used to in yer ain hoos, eh, James?' Aunt June winked at her nephew, and introduced James to the rest of the family.

As well as Uncle William—who insisted on being called Uncle Wullie—there was John—Robert's twin brother, Billy, and finally, Lily, the youngest member of the family. James was a little relieved that Aunt June had not introduced him to Billy again, as his cousin's face looked bitter as vinegar.

'Mum! Mum!'

James flinched in fright as a young girl burst into the house. Her cheeks were ruddy and her hair a wild mess.

'Alice! What is it? What's wrong?' Mrs Harkins asked.

'Mum! I'm a *weaver*! It's a *tiny* wee loom, but it makes this cloth. And I have to go back. And Mrs Moir said...'

'Alice! Stop! Ye're makin' no sense! Sit down, take a breath, and start at the beginnin'.'

Alice sat, as the rest of the household waited to hear her story.

'Well, I got to the mill on time, and I was put in with the piecers.'

'A piecer? No' bad!' said Robert.

'Ssssh!' the family hissed.

'So, a man told me I had to go and get a "Long Stand", and I didn't know he was playing a trick on me. Then the supervisor, Mister Caley, shouted at me for wasting time, so I ran off and ended up in a wee weaving room.

'One of the weavers, Janet Moir, said she'd been waiting for a trainee and they hadn't shown up, so I would do! Then Mister Caley came in and told me to go back down to the piecers, but Mrs Moir told him to get lost! She said she'd tell Eddie Cox on him if he took me away, and that I was the best trainee she'd ever seen, and that I was a born weaver!'

James jumped again, as the family cheered.

'Well done, lass,' Uncle Wullie said.

'D'ye think ye'll stick at it?' asked her mother.

'I do, Mum. I really do!' Alice's face glowed.

'What a day this is turnin' out tae be. We'll be right well-off wi' a proper weaver in the house!'

As the rest of the family congratulated Alice, Aunt June placed plates in front of everyone. She dropped a handful of cutlery onto the table; James was taken aback as the family scrambled to grab at the knives and forks.

Aunt June brought a large pot to the table and doled out huge spoonfuls of yellow potatoes. She was followed by John, who splashed a ladle of brown goop onto the plates.

What is this? James thought.

'Right, you lot, get that eaten. Dig in, James. It's no' the best mince ye'll ever have had, but hey—we're at war, eh?'

James lifted his fork and hesitantly scooped up a mouthful of potatoes. They tasted watery and plain. He looked around the table, but couldn't see any butter. The rest of the family ate with great gusto, and before long, even James had cleared his plate.

When they had finished eating, Aunt June shooed everyone out of the cramped kitchen. Billy, still lost in a huff, stormed back to his bedroom and closed the door behind him. Within an hour the twins had vanished, and Lily had been sent to bed. Alice and her mother sat in the kitchen, swapping tales of their day in the mill.

James was left in the living room, staring into the fire, as his uncle sat, reading the *Dundee Courier* and puffing on a heavily-smoking pipe. The hours dragged by before Uncle Wullie announced that it was bedtime. James's heart sank at the thought of having to sleep next to an ill-tempered and unfriendly Billy. But by the time he had dressed for bed, Billy was already asleep, his face turned to the wall.

James climbed into bed and stared into the darkness. A while later, John and Robert came into the room and they too got into the bed, at the opposite end of the thin mattress. After chattering for a while the Harkins boys soon dropped off, but James still lay awake. He was tired, but his mind raced, crammed with thoughts of the war, his father, and the new school.

In the darkness of the unfamiliar room, surrounded by a houseful of relatives he had only just met, James pulled the threadbare sheet up to his chin.

He had never felt more alone.

6

SOAP AND SCHOOL

'Get up you two! Breakfast'll be ready in five minutes!'

James jerked awake at the sound of his aunt's voice. He screwed up his eyes and blinked away the bleariness.

'Oof!' His breath exploded, as Billy jumped out of bed, elbowing him in the ribs as he went.

James rubbed at his aching side and dragged the ragged covers from his body. He slumped to the wooden chest that contained his clothes and began to dress.

His stomach churned at the thought of taking his first steps into a new school. The previous night—lying in bed—Robert and John had cheerfully discussed how Billy had been belted that day. This astounded James. At Dundee High being caned was something which caused *huge* embarrassment—it certainly wasn't something anyone would *boast* about. But his cousins had made it sound as if Billy were some kind of hero, while describing the Headmaster as a terrible monster who preyed on small boys, belting them whenever he could.

They had smiled as they spoke—in hushed, fearful tones—telling James how the school was haunted by the ghosts of boys who had been summoned to see *The Head*, and never returned.

Deep down, James knew they were only saying these things to try to scare him.

And they had!

Once dressed, James poked his head out of the bedroom door, searching for the bathroom, but there were only three doorways: one to the girls' room, one to the sitting room, and the last which led into the kitchen.

Where is it? He wondered.

'James! Come on, it's nearly time for school. Come and have yer porridge.' His aunt stopped as James's face betrayed him. 'Ye're lookin' for the toilet, eh? It's just outside, tae the left, two doors down, beside the stairs.'

It's outside? James's stomach tightened as he opened the front door and looked out at the long, open corridor.

To the left of the stairwell stood a narrow door. James slipped outside and hurried to the Water Closet. A shiver of dread ran through him as he pushed the door open.

'Oh!' he gasped in surprise.

The small room was spotless. The W.C. stood in the corner; all sparkling white porcelain, with a dark-wood seat. Against the opposite wall, a wide bowl, patterned with blue birds and fronds, sat on top of a pedestal, beneath a shining brass tap. A faint smell of bleach and carbolic hung in the air.

James stepped inside and bolted the door.

Once he was done, he crossed to the pedestal. The wash-bowl sat flush with the top of James's chest, but a rough, wooden box sat in front of it, just tall enough for a child to be able to reach the well-used tap.

James discovered a bar of *Sunlight* soap, sitting in a metal dish beside the bowl. He lifted the bar of pure, unused soap to his nose and took a deep breath, inhaling the clean scent of the bar. It reminded him of his father. Not only because they used the same soap at home, but also because he remembered—a little over two years ago, when the Great War had been a new and exciting thing—that his father had shown him an advertisement for *Sunlight* soap in the *Broughty Advertiser*.

It showed a drawing of a soldier: standing steady, rifle raised and aiming from his trench. Beside him, a man with a bandaged head stood tall and proud, gazing into the distance. Behind them both, another soldier leaned over a bucket, with a towel draped across his shoulders and his hands up to his face, as he scrubbed away.

James had always imagined his father being the tall, upstanding soldier, and his chest swelled at the thought of Captain Gunning doing his duty. But the vision suddenly shifted into the memory of him settling into that sleek, gleaming, *wretched* Rolls Royce and waving goodbye from the window.

The same emptiness which he'd felt, as the car pulled away and vanished from sight, washed over him again.

He might already be fighting! James gripped the pedestal. His breath hitched and his shoulders shook, as hot tears rolled down his cheeks.

'*Stop it. Just stop it!*' he hissed to himself, determined not to go back into his aunt's house and let Billy see he had been crying.

He forced himself to take another long, deep sniff at the bar of soap. His sobs slowed, and eventually stopped.

A loud thumping sound brought James back to reality.

'Will ye hurry up in there! Some o' us have got work t'get tae!' complained a harsh voice.

James almost dropped the soap in his hurry to wash his face and hands.

'What's goin' on, Alex?' Another muffled voice filtered through the door.

'Och, it's the wee posh laddie Wullie and June are lookin' after. I doubt he's ever had tae use an ootside cludgie before!'

It was too much for James. He turned off the tap, snatched up a ragged towel and wiped at his face and hands. Jumping off the box, he unlocked the door and dashed out of the W.C., keeping his head down.

'Aye, about bluidy time!'

James didn't dare turn to face the voice. He reached the Harkins' front door, to find the household was emptying. Uncle Wullie had already left, and the twins squeezed past James as they bundled outside, hurrying to catch the tram.

'Bye, James!'

'See ye later, wee cousin!'

'Oh good, James. Ye're back.' Aunt June sounded rushed. 'Right, quickly, eat that porridge.'

James wolfed down the milky oatmeal as his aunt turned and shouted through the kitchen door.

'Come on you lot, hurry up! Shoes and coats on. Let's get goin'!'

'Morning, James.' Alice strode into the kitchen and little Lily wandered in behind her, talking to a stuffed doll that dangled from her hand. Billy stood in the middle of the hall: his hands in his pockets, the corners of his mouth turned down.

'Are ye ready?' his mother asked.

'Yes,' Billy mumbled.

'Well dinnae stand there wi' yer face trippin' ye!' She turned to Alice. 'Right, my wee weaver, ye'll be fine goin' in yerself today?' It was not really a question. 'I've got tae take James to see Mr McDonald, tae get him intae St Mary's.'

'I'll be fine, Mum. I'm sure Mrs Moir'll look after me.'

'Aye, Janet's a decent sort. Anyway, I'll be in as soon

as I'm done. But if anybody starts anything, just you tell Mrs Moir, or go and find yer faither.'

'I will, Mum, honest.'

'Are ye done, James?' Aunt June stopped suddenly, seeing his red eyes.

She stared at him, but James forced a smile.

'Yes, I'm done.'

'Well, come on then!'

And with that, she shooed the children out of the door.

James stayed close to his aunt as they reached the pavement and crossed the High Street. Alice turned off, waving as she headed towards Camperdown Works.

'A weaver? My... Och, she'll be fine,' Aunt June said. She watched Alice for a moment, then led the boys and Lily, across a busy road and along a narrow lane.

'Ye'll soon get used tae this walk,' she said to her nephew. 'It's no' very far. Lochee isnae very big.'

James nodded, his eyes drawn to a huge smoking chimney which towered into the sky.

You must be able to see that from everywhere! He thought, then stopped as Aunt June pointed to a redbrick building.

'There it is! That's yer school for the next wee whiley.'

James gawped in shock.

The school sat part-way up a steep slope; to the left of a rutted, cobbled road, which swept on up to a tall church building. A caretaker stood by a railed, metal gate—a large brass bell held ready in his hands.

'Right, on ye go, Lily. I'll see ye after,' Aunt June said.

Lily scampered further along the road and vanished around the corner.

'Come on then,' Aunt June continued. 'Let's get ye intae the school, James!'

It's so small, James thought. *Everyone will know everyone else, and I won't know anyone at all.*

James had attended Dundee High School from the age of five, just before his mother died. It was an enormous stone-columned building, with wide, tree-dotted spaces for its playgrounds. But *this* school, although three levels high, looked tiny by comparison. Its bricks and windows were as smoke-streaked as every other building in Lochee. There were no trees, not even any grass; only bare stone, smooth cobbles, stained red bricks and dark, iron railings. A sudden stink of bleach stung James's nose.

His aunt beamed. 'Well? What d'ye reckon? It's bonny isn't it? And it's really close tae the Baths an' aw.'

James head jerked up. 'Baths?'

'Aye—the swimming baths.' She pointed uphill. 'The library and the wash-house are up there as well.'

'Oh, I see.' James nodded, the smell of bleach suddenly making sense.

'We'll have tae take ye tae the swimming sometime,'

Aunt June continued. 'It disnae matter if ye huvnae got a swimming costume. Ye can just go in wearing yer pants.'

'What?' James shuddered.

In my pants! His cheeks reddened at the thought of being seen in public, wearing nothing but his underwear.

'Doesn't make any difference,' Billy muttered. 'It's always freezin' anyway.'

'What are ye on about?' His mother rounded on him.

'Nothing,' Billy paused. 'Just that, when we go with the school, it isn't fair—the girls get to use the wee changing rooms, and we all get stuck in *The Dungeon.*'

'Dungeon? What are ye babblin' about?'

'The Dungeon! In the baths! It's freezin' and wet, and ye've got tae get changed in front of everybody.'

'Och, away wi' ye and stop yer haverin'! And ye'd better no' start complainin' tae yer teachers about it either, or ye'll probably end up getting the belt... *again!*'

'Aww, Mu-um!' Billy's voice dripped with shame.

Mrs Harkins ignored his protests. 'I'll bet *you* dinnae get the belt do ye, James?' She carried on before her nephew could utter a word. 'Anyway, that's the school. Ye'll probably be put in Billy's class, what with ye both havin' the same birthday.'

James almost stopped breathing. *We have the same birthday?*

7

BILLY'S DILEMMA

'What?' said Billy.

'I beg your pardon?' said James.

'Aye, ye were both born on the same day, only a couple o' hours between ye.'

'So, who's the oldest?' Billy asked, his voice desperate.

Billy was the oldest of all of his friends, and *everyone* knew being the oldest was better. A day or two could make all the difference—even an *hour* would be enough.

Now—with a cousin he'd never met, who dressed like a toff, and who was turning up his nose at *his* school, Billy *had* to know that *he* was the elder of the two.

'Who's the oldest?' His mother's face twisted in confusion. '*I* don't know! What does it matter? Ye're both eleven years old, and yer birthdays are on the same day. Now come on, in ye go.'

Billy flushed with anger. He dragged his feet and

trailed along behind his mother, kicking out at any stones which appeared in his path.

Then James linked his hand into Mrs Harkins'.

Another wave of anger washed over Billy. *Who did this boy think he was, holding his mother's hand like that?*

And yet, she didn't seem to mind and began laughing and swinging James's arm back and forth as they walked.

Billy had no doubt—his mother was right. James probably didn't even know *The Belt* existed, never mind having had the leather strap smack onto his open palm.

Aye, well... we'll see about that! Billy thought.

As they entered the school gates, he wracked his brain, trying to think up some weird and wonderful scheme, which could end up with James getting the belt.

'Now, we'll have tae go tae the school office t'get ye sorted, James. And *you're* comin' as well,' his mother continued, turning towards him.

Billy's mouth gaped, his eyes wide, 'Me? Why do I...'

'Because Mr McDonald says so, that's why!' His mother snapped, and shoved him towards the door.

Billy shuffled in, his mother and James close behind.

Miss McCallum, the school secretary, appeared as if she had been awaiting their arrival.

'Hello, William. Is this your mother?' she asked.

Billy blushed and nodded in reply.

'Good morning, Mrs Harkins,' Miss McCallum continued. 'Welcome to Saint Mary's. I take it this is

James? My, look at you. Those clothes are very nice!' the secretary complimented James, but as she did, she raised an eyebrow towards Mrs Harkins.

Billy caught the glance but had no time to wonder what it meant, as the office door swung open and *The Demon of St Mary's* stepped out.

'Ah! Mrs Harkins, glad you could make it. I hope the mill can do without you today?' said the Headmaster.

'Oh yes, Mr McDonald. I'm sure they'll struggle along without me for a wee while.'

Billy ducked his head, grinning at his mother's attempt to speak *proper*.

'Well, if you give me a moment or two, we can talk in the office. Would you mind waiting here? Miss McCallum, will you make sure Mr Marra's register is altered? Thank you.' And then, in a swirl of black cloak, he was gone.

'Take a seat, boys.' Miss McCallum nodded towards the chairs.

They sat down. But, as the secretary began to whisper to his mother, Billy caught a snatch of what she said.

'Does William have...?'

Do I have... what? He thought. *What am I supposed to have done now?*

He cringed at the thought of visiting the office again. That was where Mr McDonald had belted him the day before.

He stared at the floor, thrust his hands into his pockets and slumped in his chair, feet wide apart. His eyes darted from the Headmaster's door, to his mother and Miss McCallum—who were obviously plotting *something* at the bottom of the stairs—to his cousin to see what he was doing.

None of my class had better see me with him. I mean, what does he LOOK like, with those shiny shoes?

Jealousy gnawed at him. Everything *he* had ever worn had been handed down from his brothers. And even some of *those* clothes, he was certain, had been bought from Mr. Kelbie, the *Raggie*—the rag and bone man who rode his horse and cart through Lochee every Thursday.

But, whenever Billy complained about the holes in his trousers, or socks, or jerseys, the twins would tease him. Their clothes were little better, but they loved to remind him that even his *underwear*, had at one time been theirs.

He snapped out of his thoughts as his mother dropped into the chair between himself and his cousin.

'William Harkins, sit up straight!' she barked. 'Look at James. He's no' spread out like a pound o' mince!'

Before Billy could reply, the dreaded door opened, and Mr McDonald ushered them into his office.

The room was crammed with books and glittering silver trophies. A photograph in a golden frame sat upon a huge wooden desk. But to Billy it was still the dark, dull cave where Mr McDonald lurked, ready to deal out harsh punishments to poor, innocent boys.

The Headmaster motioned towards three chairs at the front of his desk.

'So, this is James?' he said, as the visitors took their seats.

'Yes. Me. I'm James. Yes, sir.'

When his cousin spoke, Billy looked aghast, as something impossible happened.

Mr McDonald smiled!

'Well, James, welcome to Saint Mary's. It is a little unusual to be enrolling someone on a Friday, but I fully appreciate the reasons why. I understand you were at the High School before?'

James nodded, as Mr McDonald continued.

'You will no doubt find we do some things quite differently here. For one, although the playgrounds are separate, we do not have a girls' school as such, so you may be forced to *talk* to the young ladies now and again.'

Billy gawped in disbelief as Mr McDonald smiled again. Even worse, his mother and the posh boy smiled *back*, as if it was the most natural thing in the world!

Who *was* this man sitting in front of them, making jokes about talking to girls? Where had *The Demon of Saint Mary's* gone?

Billy abruptly realised the room had gone very quiet, and that every eye had turned to him.

'Well? Answer the Headmaster, William,' his mother said. 'Are ye goin' to look after yer cousin?'

'What?'

'I said, I am certain that you will do your best to help James settle in quickly, William,' Mr McDonald said, quieter than Billy had ever known him to speak.

Billy's face turned pale. The floor beneath him seemed to shift and yawn.

He had to take care of this wee snob? This *toff*? It wasn't *fair*. He didn't even *like* him! But the gaze of The Head and the stare from his mother—whose eyes were narrowing in a deep frown, the longer that Billy sat and said nothing—were too much for him.

'S'pose so,' he muttered.

'Good!' Mr McDonald said. 'Then you can both go straight to class. Your mother has papers to see to.'

A moment later, James and Billy were back outside the Head's office. They stood in a sullen silence; James not knowing where to go, and Billy unwilling to talk to his cousin.

Miss McCallum poked her head out of her office. 'Are you done, boys? Better get off to class then.'

'C'mon,' Billy mumbled and stalked off down a bare, stone corridor toward his classroom.

It was going to be a long day.

8

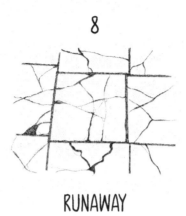

RUNAWAY

As soon as Billy opened the classroom door, his teacher called to both boys.

'Harkins, get to your seat. Gunning, over here, please.'

James's heart sank. He inched to the teacher's desk, while Billy trotted to his seat.

'The rest of you, get on with your arithmetic.'

The clatter of desk lids filled the room.

'So, James Gunning, yes?'

'Yes... yes, sir,' James replied.

'Age?'

'Eleven, sir.'

Mr Marra scribbled notes into a large leather-bound book. 'And you're currently living with the Harkins? Your aunt and uncle?'

'Yes, I am, sir.'

'Address?'

'I... I don't know, sir.'

The rest of the class burst into laughter. James flushed, but Mr Marra leapt to his feet.

'Silence!' he bellowed. 'You should be preparing for today's work. Not listening to a conversation I am having. That is the very *height* of rudeness.'

The class fell silent.

Mr Marra sat again and continued as if nothing had happened. 'Now... Address... I can get that from your cousin's records, I suppose.' He closed the book and placed his pen into its inkwell.

'So, James, I am Mr Marra. I'll be your teacher for as long as you are with us. How's your reading and writing?'

'I think it's quite good, sir,' James said. 'I can use a dip-pen, and I read *Treasure Island* and *Alice in Wonderland* to my father last year.'

Mr Marra's eyebrows rose slightly. 'Very good. And what is twenty-six multiplied by three?'

James opened his mouth at the sudden question. For a moment, his mind went blank, then he closed his eyes and thought for a moment.

'Seventy-Eight?'

A smile flickered across Mr Marra's mouth.

'Very good, Gunning. Go and take a seat.'

James almost ran to the back of the classroom, avoiding the curious stares from the other children. He slid behind his new desk and gazed around the room.

The rough desks and chairs, the faded blackboards, even the chipped writing slates—everything looked old and worn. Mr McDonald had been correct—there were many differences between St Mary's and Dundee High.

For an hour or so James hesitated to join in with the lessons. But after a while, he began to raise his hand, as Mr Marra asked questions of his pupils.

But then the playtime bell rang.

As the class emptied into the playground, Billy took off with three or four other boys, barging past his cousin, who stayed close to the playground wall.

James watched, as boys clustered on their hands and knees around a roughly drawn chalk circle, happily squabbling and flicking marbles at each other. Another group played Tig—although it seemed to James that at least three people were *IT* at the same time. Some boys rolled hoops. Others lashed out with the rods from their spinning tops. And all of them shouted and laughed, as they ran around like a pack of stray dogs. But whenever James's eyes met those of another boy, most glanced away. Others laughed, and some pointed at him before turning back to giggle with their friends.

A dark mood crashed down onto him. *It isn't always going to be like this, is it? What's wrong with me?*

His heart sank further, as Billy came strutting across the playground with another three boys in tow.

'See!' he crowed to his friends. 'I told you. Look at

him. Look at his *trousers!*'

'Hey! Nice shoes, *Posh Boy!*' One of them cackled.

'Aye,' Billy said, almost doubled up with forced laughter. 'Hey, Kevin, you should baptise them for him!'

One of the giggling mob moved towards James, his hands held together, as if in prayer. James tried to step backwards, but the playground wall stopped him short.

'Oh, *God of All Small Boys*,' Kevin spoke in a deep and serious voice. 'We ask that you smile down upon us, and give us your blessing, as we name these shoes... DIRTY!' The low voice changed to a screech, as Kevin dragged the sole of his boot across the top of James's left shoe.

The other boys almost collapsed in faked hysterics as Kevin re-joined them. All four staggered off, holding each other for support.

James's eyes welled up. Dark grey scratches cut into the shoe leather, the shining black surface now coated with a layer of dust and dirt.

It's nothing. It's just a shoe. It's not important.

He screwed his eyes closed and clenched his fists. *Everything* was ruined. His father had gone, his friends were gone, and Mary and Toosh were gone. Aunt June's house was so full of people that James could easily get lost among them. And his cousins—or Billy at least—seemed to want *him* to be gone.

As he wiped away his tears, a bubble of anger burst in his brain. *I should just leave!*

The thought came with such force that it stopped his tears dead. James glanced around the playground as a dozen ideas jumped into his head all at once.

Could I really just walk out of here and get back home? How will I get into the house? Mary and Toosh won't be there.

He knew it was a ridiculous notion, but if he *could* make it back, the pantry would be well stocked, with more than enough food to keep him until Christmas— and everyone said the war would be *over* by then.

It was silly—even a little scary—but all he had to do was walk out of the main gate, and... *Then what?*

He didn't know. But the longer he stood by the gate, the more he wanted to leave. James glanced around the playground and stepped through the gate. He tensed, waiting for some cry or shout to ring out, ordering him to get back inside. But no-one did.

He broke into a run, bolting up the small, steep road. He passed the wash house, with its stifling stink of bleach, and reached the top of the hill.

James darted across roads and tramlines, dodged through the crowds of people who milled by the tenements and shops. He ducked into narrow alleys, following worn, cobbled roads. He ran and ran, until he could go no further, and slumped against the wall of a tenement block, heart hammering and his breath coming in hot, hard gasps.

After a few minutes, he pushed himself from the wall and scanned the sights around him. Nothing looked familiar.

Panic gripped him.

I'm lost!

A shabby tenement block stretched off into the distance, but the street was strangely empty of people. It was the quietest part of Lochee James had seen.

He forced himself to move and crept alongside the dark stone building. Then something caught his eye. Something huge, which towered into the sky.

It's the big chimney! That's where Aunt June works!

All thoughts of trying to get back to Broughty Ferry flew from James's head, replaced by the image of the red-brick tower. The chimney would help him find his way back to his aunt's home. Everything would be fine.

He followed the street, heading toward the smokestack, but the road soon curved away and led into a dank, narrow alley. In the gloom, the buildings appeared to lean into each other, and James stretched his neck, turning his face upward, searching for the slightest glimpse of the chimney as he moved along pavements made more of cracks than of stone.

'Ooof!'

James bounced off of something. He spun and hit the ground, landing in a puddle of sour smelling liquid. His head cracked against a wall, and a broken paving stone cut into the palm of his right hand.

'Hoi! What're ye playin' at?'

James turned towards the voice, but his vision had blurred. A dark shape loomed over him.

'I said, what're ye playin' at, laddie? Were ye tryin' to pinch my wallet?'

The coarse words cut through James's dizziness.

'No!' James tried to shout back, but his voice emerged only as a whisper. 'I didn't! I wouldn't...'

The man reached out a huge hand. 'Right, I'm takin' ye to a Boaby! Wee thieves like you should be in the jail!'

Jail?

James scuttled backwards, rolling away from the grasping hand.

'Hey!' The man yelled. 'C'mere, ye wee beggar, ye! THIEF! THIEF!'

That single word wiped away James's weariness, his need to find the chimney, and all thoughts of his home. They were all replaced by the absolute knowledge that thieves were sent to jail. James *knew* he'd done nothing wrong, but he also knew no-one listened to children.

He sprang up from the pavement and ran.

The soles of his feet stung as he fled, his head down, hurtling around corner after corner. He had no idea where he was going, or even if the angry man was following, but he ran on, twisting and turning into unknown streets and lanes, until a stabbing pain gripped at his side.

He clutched at the sudden cramp. His steps faltered into a stumbling walk, as he lifted his head to find a huge, black gate standing before him. Set above the welded metal, in tall, iron letters, were the words *Camperdown Works*.

Beyond the gate, a massive chimney rose to the clouds.

Tears of relief ran down his face. He wiped at his eyes, with a hand that oozed blood, and slumped through the gate. Long, high, window-filled walls hemmed him in, and a muffled, rhythmic thump, like the heartbeat of a million giants, surrounded him.

A door opened and a man strode out and grabbed James by the collar. He lifted his tired arms in a weak attempt to protect himself, as the man began to rant.

'What d'ye think ye're doing! Ye cannae go intae the weaving sheds wi' all that blood on yer face! Ye'll be lucky if Mr McIntosh disnae gie ye a hidin' before he sacks ye!'

James's head spun like a top. He stared at the squealing, gap-toothed mouth, but the words meant nothing. The world tilted, the chimney swung in the sky, and James slipped to the ground. The shouting mouth stopped mid-word and began to make strange noises.

As the world drifted in and out of focus, another voice floated into James's dazed head—a distant, familiar one.

'James? Is that *you*?'

Then everything went dark.

9

HOME AGAIN

'How're ye feelin', James?'

James cracked one eye open. A flickering candle cast shifting shadows on the ceiling above him. He squinted against the light and tried to focus on the voice.

'What? Where am I?' he slurred.

'Ye're back here, James. Back in bed, at Auntie June's.'

'Oh,' James whispered. He moved to sit up, but a thousand aches made him groan and slump back down. His right hand throbbed to the beat of his heart.

'Now, now.' Aunt June leaned over him, shifting the blanket so that it came up to his chin. 'Just you stay where ye are. Ye've had a bit o' a busy day, eh?'

James nodded.

'Ye gave me a right scare, so ye did. All covered in blood! And your good clothes all torn! But still, ye've had a wee sleep, I've cleaned yer hands, and I even gave yer face a bit o' a wash.'

'What time is it?' James whispered.

'It's nearly tea-time. Will I bring ye a plate through, or d'ye want tae come intae the kitchen?'

'Can I come to the kitchen? I feel a bit dizzy lying down.'

'Aye, come on then. Canny though, take it slow.'

Aunt June helped James sit up. Every muscle in his body protested, but he forced himself to stand. The room shifted with him, and he grabbed at the metal bedframe and held on until the dizziness faded away.

'Better?' asked Aunt June.

'Yes, thank you,' James said.

With his aunt's arm linked through his, they shuffled into the kitchen.

'Well, well, well! It's the Happy Wanderer!' said Uncle Wullie. 'Feeling any better?'

'A bit, yes.'

'Good, good. Now, Me and yer Auntie June have had a wee word with Mr McDonald, and he promises he's no' goin' to belt ye, or send ye tae *The Mars*,' Uncle Wullie smiled.

James was too weary to smile back. He lowered himself into the nearest chair. Only then did he realise he was wearing nothing but a long nightshirt.

'Oh. Where are my clothes?' he asked.

'Aye, well. They'll maybe take a wee while getting

mended, James. They were in a right state, so they were.'

James didn't have the energy to ask what had happened to them.

The rest of the family wandered into the kitchen as Aunt June served out their meal. James's stomach growled, as if he hadn't eaten for days.

'Well, James, apart from yer wee adventure, how was the school? Did ye like it?'

'Oh, yes,' James said, forgetting his manners, and speaking around a mouthful of something his aunt called "fish sausages".

'Did Mr Marra look after ye well enough?' his aunt asked.

'Yes, he did. I got a desk, and he gave me a slate and chalk, and then I had to show him how I could use a dip-pen. I did some sums and...' James fell silent for a moment. 'Aunt June?'

'Aye, James? What is it?'

His eyes filled with tears. 'I'm sorry,' he whispered.

'Och, dinnae be daft,' she gave her nephew a soft smile. 'Ye got a wee bit scared, and a wee bit silly. We're hardly goin' tae send ye tae the poorhouse for that!'

As Aunt June cleared the table, the rest of the family began to chat about their day.

All but James, who stayed quiet, too drained to say much at all. And Billy, who kept his eyes firmly fixed on the kitchen table.

⚜ ⚜ ⚜

Billy had grinned when he heard that James was upset at his clothes being ruined. But that pleasure drained away when he learned James would be allowed to stay in bed all weekend. And it got even worse when Monday morning rolled around, and his mother burst into the bedroom and dropped a tangled bundle of fabric on top of James's legs.

'Here ye are, James,' she said. 'Ye can wear this lot just now.'

As his cousin separated the bundle, Billy glowered— some of the clothes were *his*!

At least the wee posh boy'll have to look like the rest of us now. Billy tried to console himself.

At school, he ran to whisper to his friends, complaining that James had stolen his clothes. For the next two days Billy kept a close watch on his cousin. And if ever any boy looked like they might go to talk to him, Billy hurried to distract them, or lead them away.

He couldn't do much about Mr Marra praising his cousin during class-time, but he used that same praise as ammunition against James—grumbling to his friends that the snobby interloper was trying to make them all look stupid.

It was a hard couple of days, but Billy found the

unhappy look on James's face well worth the effort.

On Tuesday evening, his mother sent Alice to the butcher, and made her take Lily and James along. As soon as they left the house, she called Billy to the sitting room, and sat him by the fire, in his father's chair.

'Right, you,' she began. 'What's the story wi' you and yer cousin? Ye've no' said a word tae him since he got here.'

'I dunno,' Billy mumbled.

He fidgeted. No-one but his father sat in this chair. It was too strange to be sitting there. And although his mother appeared angry, she spoke far softer than Billy expected her to.

'Look, son, ye cannae ignore him for the rest o' yer life.'

'Well, when the war's over, he can go back to his *own* house and I won't *have* to speak to him,' Billy reasoned.

As he spoke, his mother's eyes lost their focus and the corners of her mouth drooped. 'Oh, Billy,' she whispered.

'What is it, Mum?' a finger of fear touched the back of his neck. 'What's wrong?'

'Son. Ye cannae…' Her words faltered, and she took a deep breath before continuing. 'His faither's away to the war, Billy. Naebody can tell *who* is going tae come home from that. D'ye no' remember that wee laddie Hill's dad was killed, no' that long ago?'

Billy nodded. Arthur Hill had missed school for a

week because his father—also called William—had been killed on June 12th, the same day as his son's ninth birthday. Billy remembered the little green motorcycle, the driver dressed in black, which had stopped a few closes down the street, to deliver the telegram telling Arthur his father had been killed.

'I know, Mum,' Billy eventually replied. 'And I know he's my cousin, but I don't *like* him! He's a toff and a snob. And he thinks he's cleverer than me!'

His mother threw her hands in the air. 'Och, Billy, we cannae all be clever!' she blurted out. Then her eyes opened wide and she clapped a hand across her mouth.

Billy's eyes welled up and he leapt from his father's chair. 'So *you* think he's cleverer than me as well?' he cried, and bolted for his bedroom.

His mother made to grab for him, but then let him go. She sighed and went back to the kitchen to prepare for tea-time.

10

CINEMA

That evening, James sat with the whole family as they clustered round the kitchen table. Mr Harkins finished his tea, stood up, gave a loud belch, and then blamed Robert, who blushed as the rest of the table began to laugh—all except Billy, who sat with a face like thunder.

James's mouth fell open in surprise. He couldn't remember ever hearing *his* father burp, let alone doing it so loudly—and then blaming someone else!

Aunt June rolled her eyes. 'Aye, James, they're all rude wee things, so they are.'

That only made the family laugh louder.

'Anyway, we've got a wee surprise for ye. We're going tae the pictures! There's a show on at six o'clock, so we can all take a wander along tae the Oxford!'

As one, the children exploded into happy cries and shouts. Even Billy forgot to be in the huff, and joined in.

'Will there be a Boxcar Bill cartoon, Mum?'

'Gertie! I wanna see Gertie!'

The children's voices tumbled over each other, as they danced around the kitchen.

'Right, you lot,' Mrs Harkins shouted. 'There'll be *no* pictures if ye dinnae get this place tided up!'

The children scattered, as if a swarm of bees was upon them. James ran to help Robert make the bed.

A moment later James heard his uncle's muffled voice, telling the girls that they had two minutes to get ready, or he and their mother would leave without them. Then Uncle Wullie's head poked into the boys' room.

'You've got two minutes!' he said, in a mock gruff voice. 'If you're no' ready...'

'Me and your mum'll be leavin' without ye!' Robert and John chorused.

'You two'll be lucky if ye get out o' this house alive, wi' cheek like that!' Uncle Wullie's eyes narrowed, but the smile didn't quite disappear from his lips.

Less than a minute later, in a crash of bodies and eager voices, the entire family gathered in the living room. Above the noise, Mrs Harkins bellowed, 'All right, let's go!' and they poured out of the house, down the tenement steps, and into the smoky, Lochee twilight.

Trams crossed their path, bells clanging, as they shunted through the busy streets. The hint of a cool, autumn breeze swirled around the family, rustling a tiny scatter of dead leaves.

The family followed the road, crossed onto Logie Street, and soon reached the Oxford picture house.

The Harkins children dashed inside, and a warm excitement washed over James as he followed. The red-carpeted entrance opened onto a wide foyer. Set into the wall on the right was a tall ticket booth. A woman, dressed all in blue, sat behind its window.

Uncle Wullie strode to the booth, as Aunt June spoke to the children.

'Right, nae nonsense tonight. I'm no' havin' ye showin' me up! Any bother and yer no' gettin' back, right?'

The children all nodded. James was speechless with excitement, taken in by the twinkling lights. The others were more interested in a glass-fronted kiosk at the back of the room, which was crammed with jars of sweets.

Aunt June noted where their attentions were drawn. 'Well, ye can go and have a look,' she said. 'But I'm no' buyin' anythin'!'

Before she had even finished speaking, the children ran to the kiosk.

As they clamoured at the glass, pointing out their favourites, James and Billy called out together. 'I like the sherbet best!'

They turned to each other. James, shocked at the coincidence, broke into a smile, but Billy only glowered and turned away.

'Richt, I've got the tickets,' Uncle Wullie interrupted the rabble and bundled the children into the theatre. An usher quickly showed them to a row of empty seats.

James gazed around the auditorium. The walls were decorated with a deep red wallpaper, illuminated by spluttering gas lanterns dotted around the room. At the front of the theatre, a vast purple curtain hung above a wooden stage. To its left, a white-haired man sat by an upright piano, reading that day's *Courier*.

'Have you ever been to the show before?' Alice asked James.

'Yes. I remember going with my father, a little while ago,' James said. 'There was a cartoon all about a dinosaur and...'

A flourish of music interrupted James, as the white-haired man began to play.

'Oh, here we go,' said Alice. 'Time for a wee sing-song.'

James turned his head this way and that, as some voices began to sing along to the music.

It's a long way to Tipperary, it's a long way to go.
It's a long way to Tipperary, to the sweetest girl I know.
Goodbye Piccadilly! Farewell Leicester Square!
It's a long, long way to Tipperary,
but my heart's right there.

James found himself singing along with the rest. He

knew this song well. It brought back memories of Mary and Toosh, who sometimes sung it as they wandered around the house.

It's a long, long way to Broughty Ferry, he thought.

He almost laughed at how foolish he had been, trying to find his way back to Cedar Road.

As the song came to an end, the ushers moved up the hall, turning the gas lights down to mere flickers. The purple curtain glided open to reveal a huge screen, which lit up with bright light. For the next hour the piano competed with the laughing roar of the audience, as four, short, silent movies played out.

A card reading *Intermission* appeared on the screen—and the audience again joined the piano in song.

James's face ached from smiling. The warmth of the theatre, and the sheer joy of hundreds of voices lifting in song, wiped away all of his concerns.

But then, mid-way through the chorus of '*Let Me Call You Sweetheart*', the *Intermission* card was swiped from the screen and replaced by a sombre black slide, introducing the main film.

"*The Battle of the Somme*", it read.

The music, and the audience's song, jangled to a halt. Laughter rolled across the dimmed hall, as the pianist shuffled his pile of papers and started to play once more.

Rows of waving soldiers crossed the screen. In the midst of them, marched a battalion of kilted men, which made the audience clap and cheer.

For a film about the war, James thought, *it seems awfully fun.*

But then the tone of the piano shifted, becoming deeper and slower. Lily started to cry, as the flickering images showed some dead horses lying on the ground.

The audience gasped as one, and several voices cheered, as a massive explosion threw tons of earth and sludge into the sky. An enormous hole had been blasted out of the ground and a soldier appeared in the picture, climbing up the sloping crater's side.

James's stomach somersaulted. His father was just like the soldiers on screen, living through what he was watching. His throat tightened, and his head throbbed, as fears for his father's safety crept over him.

Then, all at once, the British soldiers were on the attack. Men ran, some falling and dying before they had fully clambered out of the trenches. Others tried to run through coils of barbed wire, some dropped into the mud like discarded dolls, and didn't move again.

Never-ending lines of prisoners and wounded men tramped across the screen.

The cheering from the audience had stopped, and the sound of weeping could be heard, as they watched more shelling, more walking wounded, more corpses and prisoners.

Then—in the midst of the smoke and death and

chaos—the scene changed to show a river. Hundreds of soldiers lined its banks and were washing in the stream.

'Ye see that, William Harkins! I never want t'hear another excuse from ye!' Aunt June's voice filled the theatre. 'If they soldiers can have a wash in the middle o' the war, then *you* can scrub behind yer ears *any* day o' the week!'

The audience around her burst into laughter and Billy sunk down in his chair, embarrassed beyond words. But he soon rose again, cheering wildly, as another platoon of kilted soldiers marched by in formation.

The piano played a final few chords and a map showing the British advance flashed onto the screen, quickly followed by a black card reading *The End*.

As the ushers walked through the hall, turning up the gas lamps, the purple curtains closed and the audience began to leave. James still sat, staring at the stage, thinking only of his father.

Aunt June led the children back outside. It had grown dark, and a little colder. Two women stood by the cinema doors, holding white feathers. They ignored the family as they began to walk back along Logie Street.

'Who were those women?' James whispered to Alice. 'And what were those feathers for?'

Alice rolled her eyes. 'Well... there's a bunch of women who call themselves *The Order of the White Feather*. They hang around places like pubs or football matches, and they give feathers to men who aren't in uniform. They think that men who don't go to fight are cowards, and they use the white feather to say it. They didn't try to give Dad one, 'cos everyone knows he has a bad leg.'

'Oh.'

James hadn't thought that some men wouldn't want to fight in the war. But, if nothing else, the movie had shown him that war looked scary. He had always known that people were killed in battle, but the pictures in the film had made it *more* real to him. He couldn't imagine what it must be like—actually being there.

Those men going 'over the top' must be so brave. He thought with a shudder.

That evening, James tried to ignore Billy as he prattled on to the twins about the mortars and the rifles and the bayonets of the "*Brave Scottish Soldiers* fighting against the *Evil Germans*", of the crashing of bombs and guns and explosions, and how "millions of *The Hun*" had been taken prisoner. All for King and country.

He was still talking about it by the time they went to bed.

But, as James drifted into sleep, the only thought that stayed with him was that war—no matter what some might think—was not a game.

11

McLINTOCK

At school the next day, during playtime, James watched as Billy rounded up his friends. They stamped around the playground, arms slung across each other's shoulders, calling out, inviting others to come and join them.

Before the Harkins visited the cinema, this cry had always been a call to play at *Cavalry and Indians*, but Billy had altered the song, and a line of boys marched back and forth, shouting:

'*Who wants a game at Bri-tain Ver-sus Ger-ma-ny?*'

As the line grew longer and longer, the chant became louder and louder.

Playing that game was the last thing on James's mind. The very thought of it made his skin crawl, yet he still watched, as the meandering march broke up into a scattering of twenty or more boys, who spread out and ran in wild circles.

Every boy became a soldier. They aimed invisible rifles, shot invisible pistols, and threw invisible grenades. Some pretended to ride horses, while others drove motorcycles—and all fired enthusiastically as they went.

After a while, some screamed—striking dramatic poses as they did so—before crumpling to the cobbles. They twisted and writhed in dramatic fashion, dying upon the dusty playground, until they were tagged by another boy and miraculously returned to life.

The battle drifted towards James, as one of Billy's friends, the one called Ben, backed away from an approaching enemy—smiling and firing all the while.

Then, from out of nowhere, a larger, black-haired boy jumped in front of Billy's friend. He made his hand into the shape of a gun and jabbed his fingers into Ben's ribs.

'BANG!' he yelled. 'Gotcha, ye dirty Jerry!'

Ben fell backwards and landed hard.

'Ow! Stoppit! That was sore! You're not even *playing*!' he cried, and tried to get up.

But the other boy kicked out with the sole of his boot. It caught Ben in the shoulder and sent him back down to the cobbles.

'Come on then, Jerry! Up ye get! Are ye no' goin' tae fight? Aww… are ye goin' tae greet for yer mammy, and tell her that yer fightin' for the Jerries, are ye?'

Ben, clutched at his shoulder. Tears fell, making streaks upon his dirty face, but he still shouted back.

'Don't you say that! My daddy's fighting in the war. My daddy's there *right now!*'

His cries struck at James. *Of course! Some of Billy's friends' fathers must also be off to the war.*

'Aww, the poor wee laddie,' the bully's voice mocked. 'His *daddy's* away tae the war. His *daddy* isnae goin' tae come back! His *daddy...*' he got no further, as James ran over, and shoved him away from Ben.

'Leave him alone!' James shouted.

The tall boy stumbled backwards, his eyes wide with shock, but he quickly shook it off.

'Hey, would ye look at that. It's the wee toff!' He smiled nastily at James. 'Beat it, you. Or I'll *batter* ye!'

James swallowed, his throat dry as dust. All around him, the shouts and screams of the other boys became fainter, as they noticed that *something* was happening.

'I said, *beat it!*' the bully stepped forward, his fists clenched tight.

'No,' James said, surprised at how brave his voice sounded. 'Go away. Ben didn't do anything to you.'

'Oh well, if ye put it like that...' the dark-haired boy shrugged and began to turn away. But then his hand lashed out and smacked into the side of James's face.

James spun. His arms whirled like pinwheels as he fought to stay on his feet. Tears sprang to his eyes. He wiped them away to see Ben scuttling backwards, as the bully moved toward him. James lunged forward and slammed his shoulder into the tall boy's side. The bully tumbled and landed in a heap on the ground.

A taste of warm metal dripped onto James's top lip. He wiped at his nose, and his hand came away streaked with blood. He rubbed the red onto his trousers as he moved to stand beside Ben.

The bully stood up and made a great play of dusting himself down, as another boy ran to stand beside him... then another. The bully turned to face James.

'Oh, you're dead, so ye are!'

All three took a menacing step towards him.

'James,' Ben hissed from the ground behind him. 'James, run. That's McLintock and some of his gang. They'll batter you. Just run.'

Every bone in James's body screamed at him to do exactly that. But instead he gritted his teeth and clenched his fists. He had no idea what he was going to do, but he would not stand by and let Ben be picked on.

'I'm goin' tae *murder* you, ye wee...' McLintock stopped. His eyes darted from side to side.

'Beat it, McLintock!' Billy's voice came from behind James. His skin prickled; he was dying to turn around, but didn't dare take his eyes from the boy in front of him.

McLintock looked beyond James and, for a second, his eyes flickered with something like fear.

'What? Ye think ye're big enough, do ye, Billy Harkins?' He twisted his face into an ugly sneer. 'Is it a rammy yer wantin', is it? *Well, come on then!*' McLintock almost screamed, as he and his friends squared up.

James tensed, as Billy and two of his friends marched past him, and stopped a few feet away from McLintock.

For a full minute, the two groups threw the foulest of insults at each other, using words James had never heard in his life. He didn't know what most of them meant, but they sounded harsh and cruel.

'COME ON!' McLintock yelled again, and he and Billy raised their fists and stepped towards each other.

Then a boy came hurtling towards them. 'John! John! *Mad Jock's* comin'!' he yelled.

McLintock dropped his fists. He pointed at James, his face still set in a rictus of anger.

'I'm no' gonnae forget this, *posh boy!*' he snarled, then turned on his heel and walked away, as Mr Ferguson, the history teacher, came strolling through the school's main door—unaware of the slaughter he had prevented.

Ben leapt to his feet. 'Did you see that?' he said. 'Your cousin punched McLintock in the head!'

James opened his mouth, about to say that he had only *pushed* McLintock, but Billy and his gang were already ushering Ben away.

James pulled a handkerchief from his pocket and dabbed it against his nose. It came back spotted with bright red blood. He was alone again, standing at the edge of the playground, as the crowd of curious onlookers drifted back to their games.

* * *

Billy laughed, as he and his friends marched across the playground. 'How funny was that? McLintock whacked my stupid cousin right in the face! Honestly, he's a total softie. We all went to see *The Battle of the Somme* last night. And he started bubbling during it.'

'Hey! *I* saw that as well, and *I* was greetin' too!' Ben complained. 'It's easy for you, Billy Harkins, your dad isn't away to the war.'

'It's not my *dad's* fault that he's got a gammy leg!'

'At least *James* came to help me! Nobody else did!'

'Whit? Who was it that was away to fight McLintock?'

'To be fair,' Derek put in. 'Your cousin *did* stop McLintock from battering Ben.'

'Pffft,' Billy waved a hand. 'He would've run away.'

'I...' Ben began, but Kevin interrupted him.

'Lads,' he said, sagely. 'All that matters is that McLintock and his cronies were sent packing. *The God of All Small Boys* has given us a great victory today!'

Derek shook his head. 'You know, I can *never* tell if you're serious about all that stuff.'

Kevin's only reply was a deep shrug, and a wide grin.

The four boys headed back into the school, the subject of James totally forgotten.

12

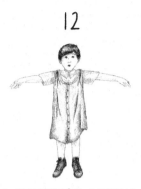

A RECKITT'S SPECIAL

It didn't take long for James's nose to stop bleeding, but the smack to his head had raised a bruise by his left eye. When the boys came in from school, Aunt June rounded on Billy, demanding to know what had happened, her tone suggesting it had somehow been Billy's fault.

Billy shouted back that it didn't have anything to do with him and that he hadn't even *been* there.

James stood in the hallway, embarrassed, as Billy howled his innocence, while Aunt June yelled at him not to answer her back. It wasn't long before she sent her son to his room.

As Billy stormed off, clearly angry and upset, James could almost understand *why* his cousin was unhappy with him being in the house—especially if Aunt June was blaming Billy for things that were not his fault.

James tried to explain to Aunt June that it really didn't

have anything to do with Billy. But his aunt only *shush-*ed him and herded him into the kitchen.

James sighed. Aunt June thought she knew the truth of it, so it seemed nothing else would be listened to. He sat down, silent and un-complaining, as his aunt lifted a large, brown teapot from the kitchen table.

She poured the cold tea down the sink and then slipped her hand into the pot, to scoop out the used tealeaves. Dumping the sludge onto an old dishcloth, she carefully wrapped the towel up around itself, then gently pressed the cold, damp cloth against James's bruised eye.

'That'll help the swelling go down,' she said. 'Hold it there for a wee while, I'll be back in a minute.'

James held the cloth in place and closed his eyes. His face throbbed a little but wasn't too sore. A rivulet of cold tea ran down his face. Goose-bumps raised on his skin, and he shivered as the droplet travelled down his neck.

'Oh! Hello, James. Been fighting have you?'

He opened his eyes to find Alice standing by the table.

James blushed. 'No...' he replied. 'Well, sort of...'

Alice laughed. 'I hope Billy didn't hit you *too* hard.'

'Oh, it wasn't Billy. It was another boy. Ben said his name was McLintock.'

Alice gave a deep sigh. 'Really? Him again?'

'Again?'

'John McLintock. He's one of the Irish children from

Balgray Street. Him and his pals are the *sworn enemies* of Billy and *his* pals! They act as if it's the end of the world if one of their *dens* gets wrecked.'

'Dens? The places where foxes live?' James asked.

'No!' Alice laughed. 'A den is a kind of place where...'

She got no further, as her mother bundled back into the kitchen.

'Alice! It's about *time* you were home. Come and help me get the tea on. James, you can put that cloth down and get out of the way.'

James handed the cloth to his aunt and went into the sitting room. There, he found a crumpled copy of *The New Penny Magazine* and settled down to read.

⚔ ⚔ ⚔

The family had all but finished their evening meal, when Aunt June turned to James.

'Here, James, ye never *did* tell me if ye'd brought a swimmin' costume with ye.'

'Swimming costume? No. No I haven't.'

'It's just that the school goes tae the Baths tomorrow, at least, yer class does. Did Billy no' tell ye?'

'No.'

'Well, that's a wee bit o' bother.' Aunt June narrowed her eyes at Billy, who stuffed half a potato in his mouth in an attempt to hide his grin. 'There's no gettin' ye one at this time o' night, either. All the shops'll be shut. And besides, they're no' cheap, ye know?'

She turned to her daughter. 'Alice, away and get one o' yer faither's old short-sleeved nightshirts. Time for a *Reckitt's Special*, I think.'

Alice jumped up and ran out of the kitchen.

'I remember when Mum made a Reckitt's Special for John,' Robert said. 'It's a *Harkins Family Tradition*!'

'Aye, it is that,' Aunt June replied. 'Right, here's Alice back. Up ye get, James.'

Alice placed an off-white nightshirt over James's head. He wriggled his arms through the sleeves and stood with his arms outstretched. The shirt hung down to his knees.

'That's perfect. Alice, away and get me some pins.'

'Already have them, Mum.' Alice knelt in front of James and pinned the nightshirt together—front to back—between James's legs, and down the sides.

'Now, James, slide your arms out of the sleeves and let it fall down.' James did so and the shirt fell to the floor.

Alice snatched it up. 'Back in a wee minute!' she said, and skipped through to the girls' bedroom.

'Robert, put a pan o' water over the fire,' Aunt June said, and Robert jumped up to obey. James sat back down at the table, as everyone else left the kitchen. Aunt June finished clearing up and came to sit beside him.

'So, Alice tells me ye got intae a fight with that McLintock, laddie. Is that right?'

James nodded.

'Well, dinnae tell Billy I said so—but well done, you! That McLintock's just a big bully, so he is. If there's a laddie around here that's set tae end up on *The Mars*, then it's him. No doubt about it.'

'Finished, Mum.' Alice returned to the kitchen, the nightshirt dangling from her hand.

'That was quick! Well, get me the blue-bag, then.'

Alice rummaged through one of the kitchen cupboards, then came back to the table holding a small, blue and white striped paper bag. She set it down and opened the bag, as if she were peeling petals from a flower— to reveal a misshapen, solid-blue lump.

'What's that?' James asked his aunt.

'That's *blue*, that is. It helps the washin' look white.'

'Blue makes the clothes white?'

'Aye. But that's no' all it can do. Look, the pot is boilin', watch this.'

James watched, fascinated, as his aunt dumped the nightshirt into the boiling pot. She stirred the water with a large wooden stick, then dropped in the blue lump.

'Now, we leave it for a wee while,' she said. 'I'll give it the odd stir, but in about an hour, ye'll have yerself a new swimmin' costume.'

James had never known an hour to last so long, but, when it had passed, he ran back to the kitchen.

'Ah, yer just in time, James,' Aunt June said. She gave the water one last stir, then used the stick to lift out the soaking nightshirt and dropped it into a pot of water.

She let it sit for a few moments then began to wring the garment out; a stream of blue water ran into the sink.

'There ye are! How's that, then?' she smiled at James as she let the shirt hang free.

'Wow!' James gasped in surprise.

Alice had cut, shaped and hemmed the material; the neck had been split and buttoned. The old nightshirt had been transformed into a short-sleeved, short-legged, one-piece bathing suit. The most startling change was the colour. Instead of grubby white, the material had become a bright and vibrant blue.

'It's… It's very blue.'

'Aye... good isn't it?' Aunt June replied. 'Now, I'll nip tae the wash-house and run it through the mangle. Then we'll hang it in front o' the fire, and it'll be fine and dry for tomorrow. Now, away ye go—get out from under my feet.' His aunt flicked the costume towards James, spraying him with droplets of water.

James leapt away from the table, giggling as his aunt chased him around the kitchen. Still laughing, he escaped into the sitting room, and lay on the floor by the fire, and read old newspapers until it was time for bed.

13

THE BATHS

The Lochee Swimming Baths was awash with bodies. Both of the Primary Six classes from St Mary's streamed into the building and split into two large groups. The girls disappeared into a row of small cubicles which lined the edge of the large pool, while the boys were taken away— down some damp stairs, into a dim, cavernous room.

It was known to every Lochee schoolboy as—*The Dungeon*. Grim tales were told of boys who had gone down to get their clothes after swimming—and had vanished—never to be seen again!

What was closer to the truth, was that some of their *clothes* were never seen again—nor anything else of value which might have been left lying around.

'Now, boys, get changed as quickly as you can. I'll call you up to the pool when it's time.' Mr Marra bellowed across the wide room, then marched back upstairs.

Shouts and cries and clothing flew everywhere as the boys hurried to change. James undressed slowly, never having done so in front of so many people. He was glad that he'd listened to the advice Alice had given him the previous evening. After his *Reckitt's Special* had been mangled and dried, she had suggested that he put it on beneath his clothes, when he dressed for school.

He piled his clothes onto a damp, wooden bench and waited, shivering in the gloom, in his uncle's nightshirt.

'Boys! Upstairs, now!' Mr Marra's voice caused a stampede as the boys yelled their way up to the pool.

James screwed up his face in disgust, as his bare feet slipped upon the slimy, stone steps. He crossed his arms against his chest, trying to hide the home-made swimming costume. The short legs were perfect, but the neck and body flapped around a bit too much.

But his concerns about the costume faded, when he noticed three boys standing apart from the others. They stayed close to the walls, staring at the tiled floor, their faces bright red and glum as death—wearing nothing but their underpants.

James reached the poolside, to find the girls were already in the water. A rope floated in place, dividing the pool into two sections: one for the girls, the other for the boys. Every pupil had been well informed, if *anyone* crossed that rope, they would get the belt—even the girls.

A sharp whistle blew, and the small boys cascaded into the water. James was swept along with them. A flurry of splashes was soon followed by a wave of shouts and cries.

'It's freezin'!' echoed from over two dozen mouths.

'You'll warm up when you start swimming!' Mr Ferguson called back.

James bobbed into deeper water, bouncing on the balls of his feet, waiting for instructions from the two teachers. But it soon became clear that no actual lesson was taking place. The children swam around in random patterns, chasing and splashing each other. Every one of them was screaming at the top of their lungs, about the cold, the water stinging their eyes, or just to make noise.

James looked to the back wall, where Mr Marra sat reading a newspaper, ignoring the pool. Mr Ferguson strolled around the edge, his pipe belching smoke, shooing children away from the sides and calling out warnings if they strayed too close to the central rope.

Something prodded James in the back and he swirled round to find Ben treading water beside him.

'Hiya,' Ben said glancing around furtively. 'I just wanted to say thank you. Y'know, 'cos of McLintock.'

'Oh, that's fine,' James replied. 'I couldn't just watch him hitting you. You're Ben, aren't you?'

'Well, kind of. My *real* name's Andrew, but all my pals call me *Ben*. I like Treasure Island.' He gave a half-smile.

James tilted his head. *What did his name have to do with Treasure Island?* But then he suddenly understood.

'Ah! You mean, the same as *Ben Gunn*?'

Ben's face broke into a grin. 'Aye! Wow! No-one else I know has read it. But they know I like it, and they know *his* name, so...' Ben shrugged, as if that explained it all.

James half-closed one eye and twisted his face into a grimace. In his best pirate voice, he drawled, 'Arrrr... Bewarrre the Blaaack Spooot!'

Ben laughed out loud, then copied James's expression and spoke in a similar voice. 'Ye mightn't 'appen to 'ave a piece of *cheese* about ye, now?'

James laughed in turn, as Ben quoted from the book.

'I've had an idea—oh!' The smile vanished from Ben's face. 'See you later,' he blurted out, as he kicked himself backwards in the water, twisted round, and swam off.

What happened there? James hopped around in a circle, looking for whatever had caused Ben's swift departure. *Ah. I see...*

Billy was floating nearby, lying on his back, staring at the ornate roof of the pool.

I bet he doesn't even know I'm here.

Sure enough, Billy drifted off to James's side, still staring at the roof.

'Gunning!' Mr Ferguson's voice called across the pool.

'Y... yes, sir?'

'Do small boys not swim in Broughty Ferry?'

'Pardon? I... Oh... Yes, sir.' James ducked under the surface, wiped the stinging water from his eyes and began to swim properly, dodging around pockets of screaming, splashing boys.

Soon, a burst of whistles cut through the din and the children hauled themselves out of the water. James followed the shivering crowd back down to *The Dungeon*.

'It's still freezin'!'

'Why is it *always* so cold in here?'

The sound of complaining boys rang around the walls, as James returned to his changing bench—to find his clothes had gone. His face turned pale as he searched on and around the nearby benches.

Where are they? I'm sure this is where I got changed?

He spotted Billy, standing near the dungeon's entrance, grinning and nudging one of his friends. Ben also stood nearby, but he didn't look happy at all.

Before James could approach his cousin, Mr Marra came striding downstairs.

'Are you lot not ready yet? Get a move on!'

Each boy hurried, vigorously drying themselves and throwing their clothes on. All but James.

'Come on, Gunning!' Mr Marra barked. 'Get changed.'

'I... I don't know where my clothes are, sir.'

The teacher rolled his eyes. 'This again...' he muttered, turning to the mob of boys. 'Where are Gunning's clothes? Who took them?'

None of the boys uttered a word, as most of them took a sudden interest in the tiles of the dungeon's floor.

'Find them!' Mr Marra barked. The boys scattered, scouring every nook and cranny.

In less than a minute Ben's voice piped up. 'Here they are, sir!' He held a pile of soaking-wet cloth.

James's face fell. As he moved to take his clothes from Ben, he caught Billy staring daggers at them both.

Mr Marra's mouth set into a thin line.

'Right, Gunning. Wring them out as best you can and get dressed. We'll get you into an art smock or something when we get back to St Mary's.' He turned to the other boys. 'The rest of you, this will be discussed when we are back in class. Get up those stairs... Now!'

As the boys fell over themselves to follow their teacher's orders, James changed into his soaking clothes. He shuddered as the wet fabric stuck to his skin, far from happy, but at least he had been left alone to get changed.

The afternoon took forever to pass.

James sat, watching steam rise from the radiator over which his clothes had been draped. Every now and then, Ben would half-turn in his seat and try to catch James's eye. Whenever he did, the small boy tilted his head, scrunched up his face, and mouthed a silent 'Arrrr!'

Despite his mood, James couldn't help but smile. Not only because of Ben's antics, but also for the way in which he ducked his head and pretended to be working whenever Billy looked his way.

I may just have found a friend! James thought. A friend who might be too timid to speak to him in public, but a friend all the same.

As the school-day drew to a close, there was a knock at the classroom door.

'If you would, please, Finlay?' Mr Marra said.

The boy nearest the wall sprang from his desk and opened the door. An older boy entered the classroom and whispered something to Mr Marra.

'Gunning?' Mr Marra called across the room.

James started in surprise, 'Yes, sir?'

'Put your things away, get your clothes, and go with Murray to the Headmaster's office.'

'Oh. Yes, sir.' James put his workbook and slate into his desk, lifted the jute bag containing his damp swimming kit, and collected his steaming clothes from the radiator. As he walked to the door, Billy and some other boys began to chant in a breathed whisper.

'*You're in trouble! You're in trouble!*'

'Enough!' Mr Marra snapped. 'If *anyone* is in trouble in this class, it is *not* Gunning. Get on with your work.'

James followed Murray out of the classroom, as Finlay closed the door at their backs.

'So, you're James Gunning, eh?' Murray asked, as he led James along the corridor.

'Yes. Yes, I am.'

'Hiya,' the older boy smiled. 'I'm Murray Murray.'

James almost stumbled in surprise.

'Aye, I know. *Murray Murray.* It was my dad's idea; he thinks he's hilarious.'

'Don't people, well, *tease* you about it?' James asked.

'Nah, not really. I never even thought about it, until some idiots started trying to make me feel bad about it in P5. It bothered me at first, but my mum told me people only tease you because they *want* you to be bothered, so they can laugh at you when you get angry or upset.

'So, whenever anyone said something like, "*Ha-ha! Your name's Murray Murray!*" I'd just agree with them. "*Aye, so it is!*" I'd say, and they'd get more annoyed than me, because I'd stolen their joke. After a wee while, they stopped trying.'

'I hadn't ever thought of that,' James replied. But he had no time to dwell on it, as they reached the steps beside the Headmaster's office. 'Do you know why Mr. McDonald wants to see me?'

'Och, I wouldn't worry about it,' Murray said. '*Old MacDonald* doesn't ask other pupils to fetch folk for belting, so it can't be that.'

Butterflies gathered in James's stomach. The idea of being belted hadn't even crossed his mind, but now it hung over him like a dark cloud.

Miss McCallum opened her office door.

'Ah! James, good afternoon. Would you come up here, please? And Murray, could you wait there for a minute?'

Murray sat in one of the chairs outside, as James followed Miss McCallum into her office.

'Am I going to see Mr McDonald?' James asked.

'No, James. Mr McDonald has already left for the day. *I* asked for you to be brought here. I've heard about the problem you had at the swimming. So, I'll nip next door for a moment and you can get out of that smock and change into your own clothes. When I come back, I'll have something for you,' she gave another smile and left James alone in the office.

Goosebumps prickled on James's arms and legs.

I don't believe I've been left alone in the school office! And I'm going to have to take my clothes off in it!

He tried to ignore the feeling and dressed as quickly as he could. His clothes were warm, but still a little damp. James grimaced, as he pushed his arms into clammy shirt sleeves.

As he was tying up his shoelaces, a knock sounded on the door.

'James? Are you dressed?'

'Oh... yes.'

Miss McCallum came back into the room and handed James a thin envelope. Even before she could say what it was, James knew—it was a letter from his father.

The envelope looked as thin as onion skin. But there, clear as day, written in his father's handwriting, he read:

Master James Gunning,
Care of St Mary's School,
Lochee,
Dundee,
Great Britain

A dark green stamp proclaimed that it had been delivered by the Field Post Office. A bright red triangle near the bottom read—*Passed by Censor No: 1963.*

'I wonder why he sent it here,' James said.

'Perhaps it was easier for him? It arrived with the paperwork he had to complete for us.' Miss McCallum led James out of the office door. 'Now, as it's almost home-time, there's no need for you to go back to class. Would you like to leave now?'

'Yes, thank you,' James said, staring at the envelope.

'Can I trust you to wait for your aunt? Or should Murray stay with you until she arrives?' Miss McCallum raised an eyebrow at James.

James blushed. 'I promise I'll wait. I won't run off.'

'Thanks, Murray.' Miss McCallum said, 'You can go.'

'Well, see you around, James.' Murray waved as he headed back to his classroom.

A minute later, James stood by the boys' gate. He turned the letter in his hands, tracing the outline of the paper inside. His hands shook; he was desperate to open it but wanted to wait until he was back at his aunt's.

James sighed, as the muffled clang of the school bell rang from inside the building.

Time to be ignored by Billy, as we wait for Aunt June.

In seconds, every gate to the school had a stream of children pouring through it.

'Hiya!'

James jumped, and turned to find Ben standing by his side. 'Oh, hello,' he replied.

'You didn't just get belted,' Ben whispered. 'Did you?'

'No, no. I got this,' James held out the thin envelope.

Ben's eyes widened. 'Ooo! Is that from your dad?'

'Yes.'

'Aw, that's nice. I haven't had any letters from my dad for a wee while. We sent him one at the start of last week, so, maybe soon.'

James nodded. 'It can take an awful long time for letters to come and go. My father always says that the post is *awful* over the sea.'

'Does he send a lot of letters?' Ben asked.

'Yes. Well, sort of. I mean, he *had* to keep sending reports to France about the soldiers he was training.'

'Your dad's an *officer*? Wow! He might have trained *my* dad! What battalion is he with?'

The boys lost themselves in conversation, until a female voice spoke over them.

'Are we ever going to get home, Andrew?' A blonde-haired girl stood smiling at them both.

'Oh, sorry, Charlotte,' Ben said. 'I was talking to James. James, this is Charlotte, my big sister.'

'Hello, James,' the girl tilted her head. 'I hope Andrew isn't keeping you from going home?'

'Oh, no. I'm waiting for my Auntie June.'

'I'm here. I'm here!' Aunt June scurried towards them. 'My, I thought I was *never* goin' tae get away from that mill today. Where's Billy?'

'I don't know,' James said. 'He hasn't come out yet.'

'Ummm... Mr Marra's kept some of the boys back. Something happened at the swimming,' Ben said.

'If that laddie's been gettin' intae more trouble...' Aunt June began, but then the school doors burst open and Billy came running out.

'Well, bye. Must go.' Ben exclaimed and dragged his sister away.

James's smile vanished.

Well, I suppose half a friend is better than none, he thought, trudging along behind Aunt June as she started off for home.

14

LETTERS

My Dearest James,

I am writing this as I travel by train, to a final destination which I cannot name.

We will pass **XXXXX**, where most companies land. Once there, we **XXXX XXX XXXXXXX XXXXXX** right across the coast.

I cannot give any fuller details but be assured that the war is going well for us, and soon the brave boys of the Black Watch will again be doing their bit to beat back the Kaiser.

Although it has only been a few hours since I left, please know that I am already missing you greatly. I hope that you are coping well at your aunt and uncle's home, and that you will have settled into your new school by the time you receive this letter. Saint Mary's has an excellent reputation, and I am sure you will do well there.

Please give my best wishes to your aunt and uncle, and all of your cousins.

Take care, work hard, and keep me as proud of you as I already am. I will write again, as soon as I am able.

Your loving Father.

James's eyes welled up as he devoured his father's words. He read it again and again, trying to decipher the words hidden under the heavy black X's stamped onto the page. His sadness gave way to frustration. The letter had been short enough as it was. *Did they really have to make it shorter?*

He carefully folded up the tissue-thin paper, slipped it back into its envelope, and placed it into the little wooden chest with his good clothing. His eyes burned, but he blinked the tears away, forcing himself to be brave for his father.

'How are ye, James? Was the letter nice?' Aunt June's voice came from the doorway.

'Yes. Father says to say hello, and to give his best wishes to you and Uncle Wullie.'

'Aw, that's good o' him, isn't it?'

James nodded.

'Well… d' ye want tae write back tae him?'

'Write back? Yes, I'd like to. But I don't know where he is; I wouldn't know where to send it.'

'Och, that's the easy bit, James.' Aunt June moved to sit on the bed. 'All the Postie needs tae know is yer faither's name, his army number, and what battalion he's with. And we *know* all those things, don't we? It'll be no bother at all!'

'But, won't it cost a lot to post a letter over the water, Auntie June?'

Aunt June shrugged. 'As far as *I* know it's the same as anywhere else. I cannae see it bein' any more than penny.'

'Oh. A whole penny?'

'Maybe a penny hu'penny, but dinnae worry. I think we can spare a wee copper. After all, it's no' every day ye get tae write tae a soldier in France! I'll away and get ye somethin' tae write on.'

Aunt June left the room and returned a moment later with a postcard which showed a photograph of the Magdalen Green bandstand. 'Here we are,' she said. 'You get writin', and I'll get started on makin' the tea.'

James almost bounced to the dresser and hunted around its untidy surface for a pencil.

A short cough made him turn to the doorway again.

'Your Auntie June says ye might be needin' this.' Uncle

Wullie threw something toward James.

More by reaction than intent, James reached up and snatched the tiny object out of the air.

Uncle Wullie's eyebrows rose. 'Nice catch! We'll have tae get ye a trial wi' Dundee Fitba' Club. We're needin' a new goalie!' he said with a smile and walked back to the sitting room.

James opened his hand. He had caught the tiniest stub of a pencil—just big enough to hold between his fingers—but sharpened to a lovely point. He knelt on the floor, lay the postcard on top of his clothing chest, and lifted the pencil. As he did, two loud, familiar voices rose from the kitchen.

'But, Mum, he's speaking to Ben!' Billy yelled, over a clatter of pots and pans.

'He can speak tae whoever he likes! It's a free country, William Harkins, believe it or no'. Ye cannae stop folk speakin' tae one another!'

'But Ben's *my* pal, not James's!'

'Well, wee Ben disnae seem tae know that, does he? Are ye tellin' me it's up t'*you* tae decide who that poor wee laddie's pals are?'

'No! But all Ben's talking about is, "*James said this*" and "*James did that.*" He's just annoying.'

'Who's annoyin'? James or Ben?'

'*Both* of them! Ben won't shut up about James, and James is…' Billy's voice trailed off.

'James is *what*?'

The kitchen noises stopped suddenly. James imagined his aunt, her hands on her hips, staring Billy straight in the eye, giving him one of her *looks*.

'He... I... It's the way...' Billy stammered. 'He's just *annoying*,' he mumbled, so low that James had to strain to hear him.

'Well, yer pals dinnae seem tae think so. Maybe it isnae *James* that's annoyin'. Maybe it's *you*.'

James gasped, and waited for Billy's tantrum to begin. But only silence followed.

'Aye, that's fair put yer gas at a peep,' Aunt June said. 'Maybe you should just away and have a wee think about that.'

The clatter of crockery began again, and Billy came stomping into the bedroom, his face a picture of young fury. James looked up, and for a fleeting moment, thought that maybe his cousin would give some kind of greeting—or maybe even a small apology.

Instead, Billy turned on his heel and left the room without uttering a sound.

'Oh well,' sighed James and returned to the postcard.

15

FIGHT!

The next day, James handed the postcard to Uncle Wullie, who slipped it into his coat pocket.

'I'll get this posted today,' Uncle Wullie said, muttering under his breath as he left the house. 'It'll no' hurt Eddie Cox tae lose a penny.'

James turned to his aunt. 'Auntie June, who is Eddie Cox?'

'What? How did *you* hear o' Eddie Cox?'

'I heard Alice talk about him before, and Uncle Wullie just said it wouldn't hurt him to lose a penny.'

Aunt June gave James an odd smile. 'Ah—aye, well— Mr Cox owns the mill, James. Yer uncle just means that he'll get a stamp for yer postcard from him.'

'Oh. That's very nice of him.'

'It is that, James. It is that,' his aunt replied, still with her peculiar smile. Then she turned and yelled into the house. *'BOYS!'*

A tumble of bodies rushed to the front door.

✝ ✝ ✝

As the children reached St Mary's, and Aunt June set off to the mill, someone grabbed James from behind.

McLintock!

James set himself to lash out, until he realised that the arms which had wrapped themselves around him were far too slim to be the bully's. They were also covered in clean clothes, and smelled altogether too much like…

Billy's wide eyes and open mouth confirmed it. James was being hugged by a girl.

The arms released him, and James turned to find Charlotte and Ben standing there. Ben's eyes were fixed to the ground, but Charlotte's face sparkled with glee, and she bounced on the spot as she spoke.

'Oh James,' she gasped. 'Andrew told me *everything* this morning. About what happened with that McLintock boy, and how you stopped him, and that he hit you, and that you *still* wouldn't leave Andrew by himself… Oh!' She hugged James again.

'Billy, you must be *so* pleased to have such a wonderful cousin! I'm so glad you're both Ben's friends!' Charlotte spoke over James's shoulder.

She gave James one more squeeze, but as she stepped

back—much to James's astonishment—another arm draped across his shoulders. He tensed, waiting to be spun round or shoved away.

'Aye, I know! McLintock thought he could pick on Ben. But we showed him, didn't we, James?'

James stared in shock. It was *Billy* who had spoken.

Billy carried on, telling Charlotte how brave *his cousin* had been, and all the while he held on to James as if they were—and always had been—the best friends the world had ever seen.

Charlotte stepped in again and enclosed them both in a wide embrace.

'Ooh! Thank you *so* much,' she said. 'Honestly, I can't thank you enough. I have to go, but I'll see you later. Bye.' She twirled around and set off down St. Mary's lane.

In a confused silence, the boys watched her walk away.

'You like her, don't you?' James said to Billy.

'No! She's a *girl*! And she's nearly *eighteen*. What makes you think I like her?'

James's mouth slipped into a sly smile. 'What makes me think you like her? Well, first of all, because you've never spoken to me so much since I came here. And secondly, because your arm is still around my shoulder.'

Billy jumped, snatching his arm back as if he'd been stung. His face turned beetroot-red.

'Shut-up!' he shouted. 'I don't like her at all! She's just Ben's sister; I've known her for ages!'

'Oh, I don't *blame* you for liking her,' James said. 'She seems *very* nice.'

'I DON'T LIKE HER!' Billy shouted.

'Really?' James kept his voice low. 'Because, you know, apparently you don't like *me* very much, but you don't go shouting about it in the playground. Yes, I think you must *really* like her.'

Billy's red face turned purple, but not—James thought—with anger. His cousin looked hugely embarrassed.

'Well, maybe *you* don't like her,' he teased. 'But your *face* certainly seems to.'

'I do *not* like her!' Billy found his tongue again. 'YOU like her!' He jabbed a finger towards his smirking cousin.

James froze, confused.

What? Of course I like her. Why does he think that liking Charlotte is an insult? What does he...?

Then he realised; this was exactly what Murray Murray had told him. Billy was looking for a reaction. He wanted James to get upset.

Instead, James took a breath and nodded.

'Well, yes. I do like her.' He paused for a moment. 'But, you know, I think *you* might *looooove* her.'

Billy exploded in a burst of ranting words—Charlotte was *old*, she had a *job*, she was Ben's *sister* and he *did not like her*!

'Don't worry, Billy,' James ignored his cousin's protests.

'I won't *tell* anyone. Will you tell anyone, Ben?'

Billy made a strangled noise, like a cat gargling honey. 'Don't you drag Ben into this!' he spat. 'He's *my* pal. Leave him alone!'

'Um… Hey…' Ben began, but James spoke again.

'Oh, of course, Billy—you tell Ben who he can be friends with—so you can keep his sister all to yourself.'

'You keep your *nose* to yourself!' Billy blurted out.

'Keep my *nose* to myself?' James replied. 'Well, all right… but at least *my* nose is *clean*. When did *you* last wash your face? Christmas?'

'When did you last *not* wash yours? Easter?'

Billy was making no sense, and a warm glow grew inside James as he realised his cousin was trying to say *anything*— no matter how silly—to stop James from having the last word.

The sadness and anger of the last few days bubbled up in James's head. The memory of every mean word, every nasty prank which Billy had pulled, washed over him. But, now that his cousin had finally acknowledged his existence, James meant to make the most of it, and if Billy wanted to trade insults, then he had caught James in just the right mood to do so.

'At least I *do* wash my face,' he slung back. 'I also have my *clothes* washed. Look at this…' he held up the sleeve of his coat. 'This was yours, wasn't it? Or was it John's? Or Robert's?'

'It doesn't matter, does it? It's *yours* now,' Billy hit back. 'You look almost as stupid in it as you do in that other daft coat you've got.'

'It's not as daft as *your* coat!'

'That's not as daft as your *face!*'

'That's not as daft as your *hair!*'

'That's not as daft as your *shoes!*'

'They're not as daft as *you!*'

'No, *You!*'— 'No, *You!*'—'Daftie!'—'Idiot!'—'Snob!'— 'Scruff!'

Their words piled on top of each other, as their voices became full blown shouts.

'Stoppit, you two!' Ben yelled. 'It's nearly bell time! If Old MacDonald catches you, you'll get belted for sure!'

Ben's words made little impact. The insults continued to fly thick and fast, until James—at a total loss for something to say—shouted at Billy:

'*Dundee Hibernian Supporter!*'

Billy's eyes narrowed, his fists clenched. 'WHIT?' he yelled and leapt at James, grabbing at his clothes.

James grabbed back and the boys began to pull each other about. Insult after insult poured from their mouths, as Ben struggled to get between them.

Billy grasped at James's hair and yanked hard, making his cousin cry out. James scrabbled blindly at Billy, caught at his collar and held fast, pulling downwards. Both boys bent at the waist, hauling at each other for all they were worth.

'*Fight! Fight! Fight!*' A cry went up. In seconds a mob of boys had gathered in a circle around them.

'Billy! James! Stop! McDonald'll give you both six!' Ben's voice was lost as the shouting grew louder and louder.

James and Billy gave out only huffs and grunts as they struggled with each other, lost in their anger, hemmed in by their schoolmates, and drowning in their shrieks.

Then, out of the blue, they both flew sideways and smacked hard onto the stone of the playground. The wild chanting stumbled into a disappointed moan, as Billy and James lay sprawled on the ground, breathing heavily, their hair like birds' nests.

James rolled onto his knees, to find Kevin and Derek standing between him and his cousin. They both glared at Billy, hands planted on their hips. With no fight to watch, the surrounding mob wandered off across the playground, grumbling as they went.

'What are you playing at?' Billy yelled. 'What did you push *me* over for?'

'What are *we* playing at?' Derek barked. 'Have you gone daft? What's going on?'

'What?' Billy's confusion turned to anger. 'What's going *on*? The wee posh boy thinks he's *it*! *That's* what's going on! You didn't need to shove *me* over. It was *him*!'

'Are you wanting Old MacDonald to belt you again,

Billy?' Kevin yelled. 'Or maybe he can just send you to *The Mars*? Is that what you want? Because even *The God of All Small Boys* wouldn't be able to save you from that!'

'And anyway... *you* started it.' Ben spoke quietly.

Every boy turned their eyes towards him.

'*ME*?' Billy scrambled to his feet and spread his arms wide. 'What did *I* do? *He* started it.' He jabbed an accusing finger at James. 'He's been nothing but bother since he came here!'

'How? How has he been a bother?' Ben stood in front of Billy. 'Ever since James came here, you've been telling us he's a snob and a weed, and that we shouldn't speak to him. But what's he actually *done*, Billy?'

Billy stared at Ben, slack-mouthed and speechless.

'*He* went to fight McLintock for me!' Ben hardly paused for breath. 'Where were *you*? I could've been *battered* by the time you bothered to come and help me!'

'But...' Billy tried to interrupt, but Ben was having none of it.

'And James didn't tell on Kevin when he messed up his shoes. He could've cliped to your mum, but he *didn't*. And *you* made him run away and get lost. Have *you* ever been lost, Billy, eh? I got lost at the Wellgate once, and a Polis-man had to take me to Bell Street, and my dad had to come and get me!

'It's SCARY, Billy! It's REALLY scary! James should've told on you, and he *didn't*. He's not done *anything* bad to you at all, and he's *not* gotten you into trouble for it. You need to say "sorry", and you need to say "thank you"!'

A heavy silence fell.

James still sat on the playground cobbles, not daring to move, but very aware that every child within earshot had turned to gawp at what was going on.

'What started this, Billy?' Derek asked.

Billy blushed and hung his head. 'He… He called me a Dundee Hibernian supporter.'

For a second, Derek's face creased in disbelief. Then he began to laugh.

'Dundee Hib… ah ha haaaa… Dundee Hibernian! As if *anyone* would support them! Ha haaa!'

Ben held out a hand to help James stand up, as Kevin's laughter joined Derek's. James had no idea what was happening, but when Ben started to giggle, he found it difficult not to join in. Surrounded by mirth, James glanced at Billy. His cousin's mouth was pressed tight, clearly trying to stop himself from joining in with the laughter.

But the others fed on their own joy. Kevin latched onto Derek, and Ben and Derek clutched at James's arms for support, as they bellowed and guffawed. Billy gave up his fight and caught at Ben's other arm, and—as natural as rainfall—all five boys gathered into a huddle, holding each other, closing their circle and throwing their laughter into the sky.

After a few moments, Kevin wiped his eyes. 'Men, you need to shake hands.'

Billy's smile slipped.

'Come on.' Derek nudged them both. 'It's about time.'

Billy kept his eyes on the playground as he slowly held out his hand. James extended his arm and the cousins' hands clasped.

They shook once.

Kevin moved like lightning, clamping his own hands around theirs—trapping them.

'May *The God of All Small Boys* look down upon this blessed union,' he spoke in his deep, serious voice. 'And may he bring you both many, little, bouncing babies!'

Derek and Ben roared with laughter, as Billy wrenched his hand from Kevin's grasp and punched him in the shoulder. James was again drawn in, as all five began to thump each other on the arm. They were all still giggling when the caretaker's bell rang, to summon the children to class.

As one, the five boys walked towards the school door, their arms around each other's shoulders, and their laughter trailing into the smoky, Lochee morning air.

16

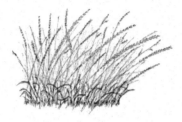

THE LONG WALK

'We've *got* to find a new den,' Billy said. 'McLintock's gang have built one at the back of the West Station.'

'Aye. I've seen it. It's rubbish.'

'But at least they've *got* one.'

'Well, *we'll* just have to find one, then!'

It was Sunday, almost mid-day. Billy had spent the morning rounding up his *men*: Ben, Kevin and Frederick—whom the other boys called Derek. A nervous, but excited, James had also been dragged along.

The boys lay sprawled on a patch of thin grass, beside the ancient headstones of Logie Street cemetery. James hung on every word the others said. He had never *heard* of dens, let alone seen one. But his new friends were determined that they needed one.

'Um… What does McLintock's den have to do with anything?' James asked.

The rest of the boys reacted as if he had poured boiling water on them. They screeched and spat out horrible, nasty names, all aimed at John McLintock. In between insults, the boys explained that their rivalry with McLintock had been going on for years—and had turned into something which Billy called "*Den-Wrecking*".

Both groups of boys loved making themselves a *den*—a hidden place, somewhere to escape from the adult world and create *Secret Boy-Plans*. And it had become of the greatest importance that if *ever* they heard their rivals had a new den, they did all they could to find it—and *destroy* it.

Billy and the others laid the blame for the conflict squarely on McLintock.

'He started it,' Ben said. 'Two years ago, we made a den beside the church, and they just *wrecked* it—for no reason at all! So, we went and found theirs. Where was that one again?'

'Beside the tram terminus. It wasn't even a proper den, just an old chair and a table with three legs, leaning against a wall. We set fire to the chair.' Derek laughed. 'Their *best* one was behind the Star Theatre, remember, the half-demolished house? They broke down one side of the cludgie's walls and leaned planks against it.'

'Aye... That's the one we got all the dog-mess for!' chuckled Kevin.

'Ewww! What on earth...?' James's face screwed up in equal amounts of disgust and fascination.

'Well, we figured that seeing as how it had been a toilet...' Kevin shrugged, as the other boys grinned. 'So, we collected as much dog-mess as we could. Alice got a jute sack, and we used big sticks to put all the mess into it. It was *stinkin*'! Then we went to McLintock's den and used the sticks to spread the muck all over it.'

'Except for Ben. He got it all over his hands!' Laughter flooded Derek's words as the others broke into giggles.

Ben raised his eyes to the sky. '*So* funny. Ha, ha. You should write for Harry Lauder,' he said, with no hint of humour in his voice.

'Wait. Did you say *Alice* had a sack?' James asked.

'Aye,' Billy replied. 'Alice used to come on raids with us, until she got all grown-up and went to the mill.'

Billy sounded a little annoyed. James wondered if it was because Billy missed his sister coming along with the gang, or if he was maybe jealous that her new job meant she could earn money for the family.

'What about Charlotte?' James asked. 'Did she ever go den-wrecking?'

'Nah,' Ben said. 'She's too old to like dens and stuff. She's been away to *big school*,' Ben dropped his voice to a whisper. 'She even had a boyfriend last year!'

Derek and Kevin giggled at that, but James noticed the smile fall from Billy's face.

'Yeah, well, Alice might not have any boyfriends, but she could climb a tree better than me!' Derek said.

'I like Alice,' Ben said. 'She's really clever.'

'Ha! She's not *that* clever,' Billy said. 'You know she just started at the mill? And you know she had someone else's birth-lines so she could pretend she was sixteen?'

The others nodded.

'Well,' Billy continued, 'after she'd been working all week, it came to Friday...'

'Payday!' said Kevin and Derek together.

'Aye, Payday. So, all the weavers are waiting for their names to be shouted out, to go and get their wage packets. But Alice had forgotten the name on the false lines—she'd done all that work, and never got paid for it!'

'Couldn't she just have found out the name, and got her wages afterwards?' James asked.

'Well... Aye, that *is* what happened. But can you not just imagine it? Standing there all, "*Oooo, I'm away to get paid!*", and then not being able to remember what your *name* is supposed to be!'

The boys burst into hooting laughter at Alice's misfortune. When their mirth died away, Billy turned the conversation back to the more important matter of finding a good spot for a new den.

James lay on the grass on his belly, resting his chin on his crossed arms. He listened to the others as they dismissed idea after idea. Their biggest problem seemed to be, that anyplace which *they* might be able to find, could also be found by McLintock and his gang.

'What if we go out of Lochee? Maybe up near Campy House?' Ben suggested.

'Are you daft? We'd get chased!' Billy replied.

'Could you rebuild one of your old ones?' James asked.

The others screwed up their faces in disapproval.

'Naah… that's too obvious,' Derek said. 'I think Ben's right, we should go out of Lochee. We *could* head up through Ardler Wood? Beside the Gelly, maybe?'

'Och, the Gelly's *great*, but there's nothing there to make a den from,' Billy said. 'Just a load of long grass and wee, bumpy hills.'

Derek sprang up, bursting with excitement. 'No! Wait! I know! Chris Moir's dad told him there's builders up at the long grass, beside the old Dryburgh quarry. We could lift some stuff and make a den near there!'

'You mean… stealing?' James gasped.

Derek waved a dismissive hand. 'Nah, not really. Just building site stuff—wee bits and pieces.'

'Are you sure about the builders?' asked Billy.

'Well, that's what *Chris* said. Up Camperdown Brae, and along a wee bit.'

'It's a bit far away, though,' Ben said.

'It's not as far as the Gelly, and we've been *there* plenty of times!' Billy reasoned. 'And if we *do* find someplace, we could stay there all day. Nobody'd come and find us.'

'Well… It wouldn't hurt to go and have a look?'

Billy leapt to his feet. 'We should go right now—we can nip home for pieces and take them with us!'

Before James knew what was happening, he was running with the pack, back into Lochee.

Derek and Kevin peeled away, as Ben, Billy and James turned into their close and ran up the stairs. Billy and James burst through their front door, almost knocking Alice over in the process.

'Hey! Be careful!' she yelped, as they darted by her and slipped into the kitchen.

Billy reappeared almost immediately. 'Where's Mum? Me and James are needing pieces.'

'She's away with Dad to see Robert's gaffer. His work's thinking of taking him on full-time when he turns eighteen. He'll be getting a *real* wage.'

'Ah! That's good. I hope *he* won't forget his name on payday, though.' Billy smirked—and then ducked, as the shoe his sister had been holding flew over his head.

'Ha! Missed!' he crowed.

'I've got *another* shoe…' Alice warned.

'I'm sorry, I'm sorry. But what are we going to eat?'

'Well, it just so happens, *Mr Funny Man*, that Mum asked *me* to make your dinner…'

'Oh,' Billy said, his grin slipping away.

'Yes… "*Oh.*" So?' she crossed her arms and stared at her brother.

'I'm sorrrryyyy,' Billy drawled.

'I should think so too. Now go and get my shoe and I'll make you a piece.'

Five minutes later, clutching wedges of bread and jam, wrapped up in brown paper, Billy and James trotted up to Bright Street. Kevin and Derek stood on the corner, leaning against the wall which surrounded St Ninian's church. Both carried similar parcels to James and Billy.

'Where's Ben?' Billy asked.

'Och, you know what he's like,' Kevin replied. 'He's always late for everything.'

'There he is. Look.' Derek pointed to a running figure.

'I'm coming,' Ben called. 'Don't leave without me!'

For a second, the boys looked at each other. Then they ran, laughing and giggling, heading up Bright Street and away from Ben.

'Awhhhh, come ooonnnn!' Ben wailed, pumping his legs as fast as he could, in a vain attempt to catch up.

The others ran to the top of the slope then slowed to a walk, breathless, but still laughing, as Ben staggered up beside them, red-faced and wheezing.

'You... you're all horrible!'

'Aw, come on, Ben,' Derek grinned. 'There's only twice as far again to go!'

Ben wailed, in mock protest, as the boys trudged northward, leaving Lochee behind them.

They eventually reached the edge of the Dryburgh fields—where the land rose steadily. Their excitement grew as, off to the east, they spied stacks of thick, wooden planks, mounds of churned earth, and careless piles of metal scaffolding poles—the unmistakeable signs of a building site. But, as it was Sunday, there were no workmen anywhere.

Long stalks of green-and-gold grass sprung from the earth, as far as the eye could see. It shifted in the gentle autumn breeze, rippling like waves, calling to the boys to plunge into it—which they all did with shouts of glee.

They ran and jumped and tumbled. Firing and bombing and screaming and dying, in spectacular leaps and dramatic poses. Even James put aside his fears for his father and leapt and shot and died with the others. But, after their long walk, a few minutes of slaughter was *quite* enough to make them all exhausted.

They trampled down a small circle of grass, like dogs making a bed, and sprawled on the ground.

A blackbird chirruped somewhere in the distance and James realised it was the first bird he had heard since he had come to Lochee; the simple burst of birdsong reminded him again of how different things were.

'Let's make the den right here,' Kevin interrupted James's thoughts. 'The grass is taller than us when we sit down. No-one'll ever see us.'

'What're we going to build it out of though, *Scotch*

mist?' Billy poured cold water on Kevin's idea. 'It'll be hard enough to find *anything*, let alone bits of wood that'll be high enough to sit down under.'

Kevin shrugged, and pulled a misshapen brown-paper parcel from his pocket. He peeled it open to reveal the doughy mess that used to be his sandwich and began eating. The rest followed his example. Soon, they were all lying back, munching squashed lumps of bread and jam, and marmalade, and cheese—staring into a sky untouched by columns of smoke or jute dust.

'What does this grass smell like?' Ben said.

'What? *Smell* like? It smells like grass!' Derek replied.

'No… I mean, yes it *does*… but it reminds me of something else too.'

'You know what smell *I* like?' said Kevin. 'When the farmers burn the stubble in their fields.'

'I've never smelled that,' said James. 'But what about the smell of a wet dog? A wee puppy that's been jumping in puddles!'

'Fireworks,' said Billy. 'I love the smell of the air after there's been fireworks.'

The boys mumbled their agreement.

'You know what smell I can't stand, though?' Billy continued. 'Jute… And it's everywhere! It's in the air, in the school, on my clothes, in the house. I *hate* it!'

'What exactly *is* jute?' James asked.

'What? You don't know what jute is?' said Derek.

'Course he doesn't! He's a wee posh boy, remember?' Billy grinned all over his face as James blushed. 'Jute's a weird plant that can be made into... like... string, or wool. It gets used for everything. Have they not taught you about that at the High School?'

'No... I mean, I've *heard* of it. I know Dundee is *famous* for it. I've just never known what it actually was. I *thought* it was a type of wool. It *is* very smelly, though.'

'Ah, you can't smell it out here, though,' Derek said. 'And listen... you can't even *hear* the mills. This is great!'

'But do you even *smell* it anymore?' James asked. 'When I first came here it seemed like I couldn't smell anything *else*! But it doesn't seem so bad now.'

'Well, all I know is that I *hate* it,' Billy replied.

'It's odd that he *can't* smell it, but you *can*,' said Kevin. 'Well, I think...'

'D'you smell it *now*?' Kevin yelled, and stuffed a handful of damp grass into Billy's face.

Billy gave a muffled cry of rage, as he spat out mud and long grass stalks. Kevin leapt to his feet and ran; his laughter trailed behind him as he bounded across the field. Billy struggled to his feet and gave chase.

Ben, James and Derek took off after them—calling to Billy to hurry up and catch Kevin—and shouting to Kevin to run faster and escape Billy.

All five boys jinked and weaved across the field until, as one, they burst into a clearing in the long grass. A half-built stone structure stood there, surrounded by a frame of metal pipes.

Ben's face lit up.

'Look!' he burbled wildly, barely able to contain his excitement. 'Look at the scaffolding! Come on! We have to go and climb on it!' he sprinted for the building.

'What?' James turned to Billy, confused.

'Ben likes climbing things,' Billy explained. 'I warn you, he'll challenge you to a race up the scaffolding.'

Ben whooped with delight, dangling from the metal bars and poles. 'Climb up! It's great. You can see into the house!' He spun around a pole and dropped to the grass.

'Flippin' show-off,' Billy muttered, unable to hide his admiration. 'I'm sure he's half monkey; he was climbing things before he could *walk*.'

Ben tugged at James's arm. 'Come on! I'll race you to the top!'

Billy rolled his eyes, so much as to say, "*told you!*" as Ben dragged his cousin away.

James's skin prickled with the new thrill of climbing in and around something that was not yet built. He had no idea what the building might be. *A berry farm? A factory? The beginning of another huge, stately house like Camperdown?*

None of that seemed to matter to his friends, all they cared about was that they had found their own, private playground.

'Are you lot coming up or what?' Ben called down from high above. 'Can't say I blame you. You're all rubbish at climbing!'

That was enough for the rest to bolt for the scaffold and work their way up the frame. They hadn't even gone half way when a voice came from below them.

'Are you lot coming down or what?' Ben squinted up at the others.

'What! How...?'

'Aye, yer all rubbish at climbing... Up *or* down.'

Kevin, Derek and Billy rushed to clamber down, calling out dire threats to Ben as they went. Ben continued to taunt them, until just before their feet hit the ground, and then he bolted. The others set after him, tearing through the long, waist-high grass, as Ben led them a merry dance over the small hillocks.

James remained on the scaffold, chuckling to himself, watching as the others become separated, as they lost sight of their quarry, and each other.

'He's over there,' Billy called. 'I can see him!'

'But where are *you*?' Kevin's voice drifted up from somewhere among the grass.

And then Ben vanished.

James blinked. *Where did he* go?

One moment, Ben had been running at full pelt, laughing and mocking his friends. The next instant he was gone. Derek, Kevin and Billy scanned the wide field.

'Ben!' Billy called.

'Over that way!' James shouted, pointing towards the spot where Ben had disappeared.

'Be-en!' the boys' cries grew more and more nervous.

'Lads! Lads! Quick! Come here!' Ben's voice rose from nowhere, so high pitched the others could not tell if he was in pain or shouting for joy.

James swept his eyes across the sea of grass, squinting against the sun. Then he spotted a tiny dark shape on the ground. 'There!' he pointed again, and scrambled to the ground, as the others ran to find Ben.

'Is it bad?' he panted, as he reached his friends.

The small boy sat on the ground: his right knee scuffed and bleeding a little, his hair full of grass stalks, his cheeks streaked with dirt—but with a smile that almost split his face in two.

'Ben. Are you okay?' asked Kevin.

'Look,' Ben nodded to his side.

'What the?' Billy said. 'How are…?' Then he saw it. They all did.

17

THE DEN

There was a hole in the ground.

It was broad and deep and long, almost a perfect square. Three small boys could easily have lain down, head to toe, and still had room to spare. At one edge the ground sloped down at a steady angle, into the pit. The other three sides dropped straight downward, and the bottom of the hole levelled off, almost completely flat.

'This is *perfect!*' Billy said. 'Look—the slope can be the entrance, and it faces down the hill. It's deep enough to sit down in, and the grass is so high, no-one will see it!'

Ben, Kevin and Derek let loose with wild yells. They jumped, and punched the air, and grabbed at each other in their glee.

'So, is *this* a den?' James asked.

Kevin threw an arm around James's neck and drew

the puzzled boy towards him. 'No, me old chum,' he said, ruffling James's hair. 'This is not "*a den*". *This* is a den and a *half*!'

'Attention troops!' Billy called. Kevin, Ben and Derek snapped to a clumsy attention. 'Our mission is to raid that building site and create The-Greatest-Den-The-World-Has-Ever-Seen! Aye?'

'Aye!' the three boys cried.

James was none the wiser, but he followed the rest as they hot-footed it back to the building site.

After a few trips they had dragged away a large sheet of corrugated iron, some strips of heavy canvas, and a scrap-end of linoleum— which they folded and stamped on until it filled the floor-space. James still couldn't decide if they were stealing or not, but he helped Kevin carry off six mostly-empty paint pots, which he insisted could be used to make fires.

'Well done, men!' Billy announced, after one last look around the site. 'Now, we should...'

'Wait.' Derek interrupted his commanding officer. 'Look at this.'

The boys clustered around a pale, jute sack. The bottom had split open, to reveal some fluffy, grey material. Derek pulled some from the tear in the sack, and gasped as it expanded into a thick, puffy wool.

'New orders, men: get this stuff back to the den!'

Billy's soldiers scrambled to grab enormous armfuls

of the material.

Back at the hole, they spread the wool all over the linoleum floor, wrapped the canvas around the corrugated iron sheet and dropped it across the top of the hole to make a sliding roof.

Kevin stuffed the paint pots with the remains of the canvas and then rummaged around in his pocket. He pulled out a battered, red box. The words "Puck Match" stood out white on the front, with a drawing of a tiny green elf, carrying the same box, on the other side.

James eyes widened. 'You... you shouldn't play with matches!'

'Och, it's fine.' Kevin waved away James's protest. 'I got them from my dad. It's easy. Look.' He drew out a match, closed the box, and struck the pale pink tip along its side. The stick flared into bright white light.

'See! It's fine!' Kevin dropped the match into the paint pot. A gutter of flame licked out, as the fabric took light.

And then the boys discovered that paint could burn.

The small flickers burst into bright yellow fire, as the sticky remains flared up, bathing the den with heat, and a shimmering orange glow.

'Wow!' Billy said. 'That is *brilliant!*'

Kevin and Derek moved the roof back a little, allowing the smoke to escape, while Billy lay down, surrounded by wool, and laced his hands behind his head.

'Ah, gentlemen,' he spoke in his best, fake, posh voice.

'Thank you *so* much for all of your efforts today. Now, if you'd just like to leave by the tradesman's entrance and allow me the peace and quiet of my little home.'

His friends' rage rattled the roof, as they looked around for things to throw at him. Finding nothing, Ben punched Billy in the arm. Billy laughed and punched him back. Soon all five boys were wrestling and thumping one another. Kevin and Derek rolled to the rear of the den, swapping leg punches, when James called to them.

'Careful! You're really close to the fire-pot.'

'Don't worry,' Kevin said. 'Look— it sits right in that wee hole. It can't fall over or anything.'

James didn't reply, but his unease never lessened— fire, after all, was still fire.

After a few minutes of beating each other up, the boys lay back on the deep, warm wool.

'Men,' Kevin said, with a contented sigh. 'I think it's safe to say that *He* is certainly watching over us all!'

Billy, Derek and Ben rolled their eyes and groaned.

'Oh no! Here we go *again*!' they chanted in unison.

James had no idea what the boys were talking about and said as much.

'Well, seeing as how you asked...' Kevin began.

The other boys started making raspberry noises, which Kevin ignored.

'You know how there's *God*, and all that?'

James nodded.

'Well,' Kevin continued, 'what most people *don't* know is, that there's also *The God of All Small Boys*.'

'Oh! Yes! I've heard you talk about that before. What *is* it?' James asked.

'He's not an *it*; he's a *him*!' Kevin said. '*The God of All Small Boys* is the one who keeps us from breaking our necks on scaffolding every two minutes, or sometimes lets us find pennies in the gutter. He's the one who grows trees, with branches in *just* the right places, so we can climb right to the top.

'*The God of All Small Boys* invented fireworks and dogs and sticks and horses and muddy puddles. And he lets us find secret places... like this!' he gestured around the den. 'Really close to a building site, where we can get stuff to make it perfect!

'He looks after us... he's the one who keeps us safe.'

Derek nodded. 'Aye, I mean, how much better could this place *be*? Isn't this just *the* best den anyone's ever seen?'

And as the boys basked in the light and warmth of the fire-pot, none could deny it... it was!

18

BLOOD BROTHERS

'What time is it?' said Ben, breaking a long silence.

Derek moaned. 'Shurrrruuuup… I'm all cosy.'

'No, really,' Ben continued. 'Does anyone have a pocket watch?'

'Derek's usually got the *world* in his pockets,' said Kevin.

Derek muttered something under his breath.

'Maybe we'd better head back. It might be tea-time,' Ben insisted.

Billy shifted sideways and lightly punched him on the shoulder. 'Trust you to be thinking of your stomach.'

'Aw, now *I'm* all hungry,' Kevin moaned.

'Me too,' added James.

'You lot just aren't going to let me snooze, are you?' Derek grumbled. He yawned and stretched, his jaw gave a loud crack as he did so. 'Did someone say something about eating?'

'I was just wondering if it's tea-time yet...' As if it had been planned, Ben's belly gave a low, rumbling growl.

'Ben's Belly Has Spoken!' announced Kevin. 'It *must* be tea-time!'

'Aye, I suppose we should head back, eh?' Billy shuffled onto his knees. 'We'll come back tomorrow after school, and sort things out a bit. But I think this is it, men! The den to end all dens!'

'McLintock would be *DEAD* jealous if he saw it,' said Ben.

A sudden gloom cloaked the boys. McLintock— they hadn't even *thought* about him, in the last, few, quiet hours.

They were far from Lochee, away from the smoke and dust and dirt. Away from the mills and trams. Here, there was a blue sky, with grass and trees, and air that didn't make you want to cough every two minutes. But, best of all, there were no grown-ups watching your every move.

But now, even James knew, all of that could be gone in an instant. If McLintock found this place, it would be destroyed—ruined beyond repair. It seemed an unwritten law—*The Greater the Den, The More it Must be Wrecked*. And this den was better than any they had ever imagined.

'We can't tell anyone about this place. Not *anyone*,'

Derek said.

Each boy nodded.

'We'll have to swear it,' Billy said.

'What on?' asked Derek. 'Our lives? The Bible? Our mum and dad's lives?'

James shuddered. 'No, I'm not swearing on my father's life. Not while he's away at the war.'

'Me neither,' Ben quickly agreed.

'That's fair enough,' Billy said. 'But we have to swear on *something*, don't we?'

The five friends wracked their brains. What could possibly be important enough to make such a solemn vow upon?

'We could… I dunno… Ach, it's stupid.' Kevin shoved his hands into his pockets.

'*What*?' the others urged him to carry on.

'Well, we could…' Kevin paused, catching each boy's eye as he sheepishly said, '… be blood brothers?'

Silence fell again, as Kevin's suggestion settled on them.

Blood brothers…

Being blood brothers was the deepest, most mysterious bond boys could ever have. It meant being joined forever in the strongest friendship there could be. Everyone knew it—blood brothers belonged to each other, because the blood could never be taken back. When you became someone's blood brother, everything changed.

James's head reeled. A week ago these boys wouldn't have given him the time of day.

He had to ask. 'I don't suppose you mean *me*, when you talk about being blood brothers?'

'Yes, we do,' Billy said, his voice strange and serious. 'This isn't the same as being cousins, James. This is more important than family. You can't *pick* your family, but blood brothers are people you choose by yourself.'

The paint-pot fire cast shifting shadows on the muddy walls. Its smoke drifted along the roof and escaped out of the den's entrance, but the atmosphere had become so heavy the boys could almost taste the air.

'Do you have your penknife, Derek?' Billy said.

Derek's face fell. 'No. My dad took it from me 'cos I carved my name on the fence beside Tony's Chip Shop.'

'Then how are we going to...' Billy's question died away, as Ben slowly pulled his hand from his pocket, to reveal a small penknife. Scratched delicately into the silvered surface was the *fleur-de-lis* emblem of the Scouts.

'My dad sent it over. A soldier carved the wee symbol onto it.' Ben paused. 'I haven't used it yet.'

'Then it was *meant* to be used for this,' Billy said, his voice hushed.

'Who's going to... you know... cut...' Ben's face turned pale.

No-one replied, until James whispered. 'I'll do it. If

you want?'

The others nodded in mute agreement, and Ben solemnly handed over the penknife. James slipped his thumbnail into a groove on the blade and folded out the glittering edge. It glowed, golden and yellow, in the flickering light.

The boys shuffled into a small circle: cross-legged, knees touching.

'Who's first?' James asked, his voice still low.

They glanced at each other, faces uncertain. Then, to everyone's surprise, Ben spoke up. 'Me. It's my knife, I should go first.'

Another silent chorus of nods followed.

'Which hand?' James asked.

'Well, the heart is on the left, so... left hand?' said Kevin.

Ben squeezed his eyes closed and held out his arm, which shook only a little. James took the small boy's hand—then a deep breath—and placed the tip of the blade against the ball of Ben's thumb. The skin parted as if it were made of silk. The boys gasped as a ruby bead of blood oozed from the thin incision.

Ben hadn't so much as flinched. He opened his eyes, as the drop of blood expanded and ran in a slow trickle down his thumb and into his palm.

'I didn't feel a thing,' Ben whispered.

'Me next,' said Billy, already holding out his hand.

James again made the smallest of cuts. Billy jerked slightly as the blade touched his skin.

'Ow...' he said, sounding more surprised than hurt. 'I felt that!'

'No!' Kevin cried, halting Billy as he lifted his thumb to his mouth.

'Oh! Oh aye!' Billy snatched his hand down.

After Derek and Kevin took their turns, the small blade was tinged with red. James could only stare at it, his hand trembling, as he held the knife over his own thumb.

'Would you like me to do it for you?' Billy asked, his voice hushed.

'Yes, please,' James whispered back.

Billy took the knife and made the final cut into his cousin's thumb.

For a moment the boys did nothing but sit in silence, watching the blood, as it seeped onto their hands.

'How do we do this?' Kevin asked.

In response, Billy held his arm out, his thumb pointing upwards. Blood oozed down its length. The others followed his lead, until each sat, arms outstretched and ready.

'Now,' Billy said, and all five boys pressed their thumbs together, each one ensuring they made contact with all the rest. Their hands became a mess of red streaks.

From nowhere, Ben spoke. His voice gentle and slow,

as if he were speaking in church.

'We are now all blood brothers, for ever and ever.
We cannot be parted, for never and never.
Oh *God of All Small Boys*, we pray,
you'll help us always stay this way.'

Kevin smiled, as the others stared at Ben in awe.

'Where did *that* come from, Ben?' Derek asked.

'I don't know. I just thought… you know… we should say something.'

The small fire chose that exact moment to cast one last glimmer of flame, before it blinked out. The boys remained kneeling in the near-darkness. None of them felt they should move, none seemed *able* to move, but eventually Billy spoke.

'We should go.'

No-one else said a word, but they uncoiled their legs, dragged back the roof, and clambered out.

'Oh. I think we've been away longer than we thought!' said Derek.

The sun had slipped low in the west. It caught the clouds, making them burn in shifting shades of pink and blue and purple. Wide, golden rays glinted back from the far-distant river. Off to the east, The Law rose from the landscape, appearing to burn in the light. While to the south the towering silhouette of Cox's Stack showed where home lay.

This is beautiful, James thought. *The sky looks so BIG.*

It seemed wider than he had ever seen it - broader even than the sky over the mouth of the Tay, where it poured into the sea at Broughty Ferry.

Down among the dark shadows of the factories, James could see small lights twinkling. Despite the distance, he was almost certain he could hear the rumble and hissing of the trams.

'This is what I meant, James,' Kevin whispered. '*This* is what *The God of All Small Boys* gives us. Who would have thought that heaven could be a hole in the ground?'

Standing on the grassy hill, his thumb throbbing slightly, as his blood and that of his brothers dried on his hand and mingled in his veins—with the land spreading out below him, and the sun coating the clouds in colours no-one would believe—if any ever dared attempt to paint this wide, wide sky—James vowed to himself, and to Kevin's strange God, that he would remember this day forever.

19

A TERRIBLE TELEGRAM

The next morning, James and Billy woke up scratching and itching. Their skin was on fire, prickling as if ants were crawling beneath it.

'Muuum!' Billy shouted from his bed, clawing at his arms.

Mrs Harkins bumbled into the room. She opened her mouth to scold Billy for not already being up and dressed. But then she saw the boys' arms.

'Look at the state o' you two! Yer arms look like they've been pulled intae a loom! What have ye been doin'?'

'Nothing!' Billy protested.

'Well ye've obviously been up tae *somethin'.*'

The boys glanced at each other. Even in their discomfort they knew; *the den must be kept secret!* But, before they could speak, Mr Harkins appeared in the bedroom, holding a tiny scrap of grey fluff.

'This was all over the back o' yer trousers, Billy. Have you boys been playin' wi' stone wool?'

James and Billy hung their heads.

'Aye, well, that'll be that then. It's no' much good for ye, laddies,' Mr Harkins continued. 'It's made from wee bits o' stone, and they can get under yer skin. And if that happens… well… ye can probably *feel* what it does. It's a wee bit nippy, eh?'

The boys nodded, still scratching.

'Gie them a wash with water as hot as they can take,' Mr Harkins said to his wife. 'Then slather them in calamine. It'll take a wee while, but they'll be fine.'

'Yer daft laddies, the pair o' ye,' Mrs Harkins wagged a finger at the miserable boys. 'I'll put a pot o' water on and ye can get washed. It'll be awful hot, mind!'

The boys continued to rub at their arms.

'This is horrible!' James moaned. 'That stupid *wool*!'

'I know,' replied Billy. 'But what about Kevin and Ben? They'd taken their shirts off when they carried it back!'

'And Derek fell *asleep* on it! They must be in agony.'

Mrs Harkins returned. 'Right, here's a wash cloth each, and some carbolic soap. Get intae that kitchen and start scrubbing.'

Both boys grumbled about the heat of the water, but Mrs Harkins ignored their protests and ensured they scoured themselves as hard as they could. Ten minutes later, the boys stood with faces like death, as Mrs

Harkins took the stopper from a large, brown bottle, and beckoned them to her. She carefully poured thick lines of bright, pink gloop onto their arms. As she smeared the lotion over their skin, the maddening itch faded.

'Ye cannae beat a wee drop o' calamine,' she said. 'This should do ye till tonight. Put yer shirts on, right now! Dinnae let the lotion dry in.'

The boys obeyed, grimacing as their shirts stuck to the greasy liquid.

'Eeew. It feels horrible, Mum!' Billy complained.

'Is it worse than that itchin'?' his mother asked. Billy shook his head. 'Well haud yer weesht, then! Now away tae school, the pair o' ye. And remember, I'll no' be gettin' ye tonight, so just come down the road yerselves.'

The boys hurried to finish dressing.

╫ ╫ ╫

As James and Billy arrived in the playground, it was immediately obvious that their friends had suffered the same fate as them. Kevin and Ben's necks were pinky-white with drying calamine lotion, and most of Derek's face had been plastered with it.

'How bad is it?' Billy asked.

'My chest, both my arms, right up my neck—look,' Ben said, pulling his shirt aside. He hardly had to, the rash at the top of his neck almost glowed.

'Me too,' Kevin said, his voice quiet and miserable.

Derek shrugged. 'You can see it. I was scratching like a dog last night. My face was all puffed up. I thought I'd get off school today, but it'd gone down a bit this morning. My dad says it was stone wool.'

'Aye, my dad said so too,' Billy replied. 'I had some stuck to my trousers. They never asked where we got it, though. You didn't tell anybody about the den, did you?'

They all shook their heads as they shuffled into school.

In class, their friends were sympathetic—at least to their faces—but during playtime McLintock and his cronies spent every minute singing made-up songs about *The Pinky Boys*.

After what seemed like an eternity, the school-day ended, and the boys trudged homeward. At the High Street, Derek and Kevin said their farewells and headed off to their own closes. The others carried on, but as they came around the corner of Lorne Street, Billy and Ben gasped and stopped dead in their tracks.

A dark green motorcycle stood outside the tenement entrance.

'Oohnononononono...' whispered Ben.

'What's wrong?' asked James.

'It's *the man-in-black*,' Billy breathed. 'The Telegram-Man.'

A chill covered James from head to foot, all thoughts of his aching skin forgotten. Ben sprinted toward the building, with James at his heels. They flew upstairs to their front doors, Billy was only a heartbeat behind James, as he slammed into the house.

'AUNTIE JUNE!' James yelled.

Billy dropped a hand onto his cousin's shoulder 'It'll be okay,' Billy said. 'I'm sure it will.' He didn't sound sure at all.

Aunt June appeared from the sitting room and reached out to them both.

'Oh boys...' she began.

Then a heart-breaking scream filled the air.

'Nooo! Daaaddyyyyy!' The voice was unmistakeably Ben's.

Billy and James bolted outside and ran along the pletty. The door to Ben's house lay wide open and the boys crept inside, hesitant, as the sound of sobbing drifted to them.

They peeked around the living-room door. A man stood in the middle of the room, dressed all in black, with a battered, white-banded cap tucked under his arm.

'...and of course the Army Council express their sympathy.' They heard him say, before he about-faced, marched past them, and left the house.

Charlotte and her mother clung to each other, tears streamed down their faces. On the floor in front of them lay a torn envelope and a crumpled slip of paper. James and Billy were at Ben's side in a moment. The small boy flung his arms around their necks. He clung to his friends—his blood brothers—and lost himself in deep, moaning sobs.

'Oh, Ben, I'm so, so sorry,' James wept, wrapped in a deep sadness for his friend. But his sorrow was tinged with a sense of relief—that it had not been his *own* father who had died. A terrible wave of guilt swept over James for thinking that way, but he couldn't help it.

Ben's older brother burst into the house, his hair wild and his eyes red. As Mrs Wilson and Charlotte stood to meet him in the centre of the room, James and Billy let go of Ben. He disentangled himself from their embrace and joined his family.

The two boys stepped back. There was nothing else for them to do or say. They slipped out of the room and left the house, closing the door gently on the Wilsons' grief.

✝ ✝ ✝

Most Lochee evenings would bring shouts, songs and yells, ringing around the streets. But The Telegram-Man had visited more than a few houses across the district; the mill-town had fallen quiet and still.

James and Billy sat in front of the fire, as Aunt June pressed tin mugs of steaming *Bovril* into their hands. James hugged the cosy mug to his chest. He'd never had the savoury beef drink before, but it warmed him and tasted good.

'I was so scared. I…' he shuddered, unable to voice his thoughts.

'I know, darlin', his aunt said. 'When that motorbike stopped outside the closie, I got such a scare! And when the man came ontae our pletty—well—I needn't tell ye, my heart was in my mouth.'

Billy stared into the fire. 'I've never heard Ben cry like that before,' he whispered. 'Not even when he broke his arm.'

'It's no' easy, son,' his father said. 'But that's the way war is. A man has tae do his duty tae the king, you know?'

'I know,' Billy replied. 'It's just… poor Ben.'

'I heard Edwina Curtis got a letter as well,' Aunt June said.

'Aye,' replied Uncle Wullie. 'Last time I saw so many telegrams being delivered was after the Battle of Loos. Somethin' bad must've happened. We'll be down a fair number in the mill this week, I think.'

The adults continued to talk in hushed tones, as Billy and James sat in silence. They nursed their mugs—watching the contents slowly swirling around or staring into the fire—and wondered on the state of their friend, the loss of his father, and the safety of their own relatives.

20

CHAPEL

When school began the next day, the number of missing children made it clear that The Telegram-Man had been very busy. At morning break, James, Billy, Derek and Kevin huddled together in a corner of the playground. A few boys gathered around the marbles circle, but most of the school reflected the stillness which had fallen over the town. All, apart from one particular group, who shouted and whooped at the far end of the playground.

'Listen to that,' Kevin said angrily. 'McLintock is making as much noise as he can. It's like he doesn't care what's happened.'

'Ignore him,' Derek said. 'He's just being a ragger.'

'I'll do more than ignore him,' Billy growled, but he didn't move.

The caretaker's bell summoned the children back to class, but as they entered the room, they found Mr

Marra standing waiting for them.

'Children,' he addressed his pupils. 'If you have brought anything to school with you, then collect it up. We will be leaving the building shortly and will not be returning today. Quickly now, in twos, line up outside the door.'

A low buzz of chatter rose, as the children filed out of the classroom, into the corridor.

'Now, P6, we are going out into the boy's playground... quietly! Christina, Finlay, would you lead the way, please?'

The children at the head of the line led the class along the corridor and out of the school's main door. Rows and rows of children followed, until the school had emptied.

Mr McDonald stood at the main gate and faced two hundred and fifty curious faces.

'Saint Mary's School,' he announced. 'In a moment we will be heading up the lane to the Chapel. You will remain in your own class lines. We will walk—we will not run—and we will remain *silent*. Do we understand?'

Every child murmured, 'Yes, Mr McDonald.'

'Some of you may remember that Lochee suffered terrible losses at the Battle of Loos, two years ago. Then, we all attended a service for the brave Lochee soldiers who made the ultimate sacrifice in this war.

'This past week, we have suffered similar losses. We will, therefore, be attending a special Mass this afternoon.

I expect *each and every one of you* to be a credit to this school, and to show proper respect for the fallen.'

'Yes, Mr McDonald.'

The Headmaster nodded to the teachers, who marched the pupils out of the school gate and up the hill towards St Mary's Church.

'Something's not right,' Billy whispered to James as they walked. 'Something's *different*. But I don't know what it is.'

'It's a bit odd that everyone's so quiet,' James said. 'It's the same as last night. The whole school is here, but you'd hardly know it.'

Billy nodded and then his head jerked up. 'No, that's it!' he hissed. 'Listen.'

'To what?' James asked.

'Everything! Listen!'

James opened his mouth, about to question Billy further, but then he realised—Lochee wasn't just quiet, it had fallen utterly silent.

No trams or trains could be heard. No carthorses clopped their heavy, iron shoes on the cobbled roads. No rumble of hand-carts or motor cars drifted from the streets. There were no cries of vendors calling to customers, and no chimneys throwing smoke into the sky. The throbbing pulse of the mills—which hung in the air every minute of the day—had stopped.

Lochee had become a desert—still and silent—under

a bright autumn sun.

The children filed into the chapel. At the far end, a snow-haired man in white priest's robes watched as the pupils and teachers filled the long benches at either side of the central aisle.

The priest stood by an altar which was draped with a purple, silken cloth, and an oddly scented smoke drifted from a small urn.

Billy dragged James into a long pew to sit down. 'Look, there's Ben and Charlotte,' he whispered, nodding toward the pews at the front of the church.

James hardly took in a word as he stared round the church, marvelling at the massive stained-glass windows.

As soon as the last child came through the heavy wooden doors, the church organ swelled. The priest motioned to the packed congregation, who all rose and began to sing:

> *Amazing grace! How sweet the sound,*
> *that sav'd a wretch like me.*
> *I once was lost, but now am found,*
> *was blind, but now I see.*

When the hymn ran to its end, everyone sat down. James—not understanding what was going on—was dragged down by Billy.

'What're you doing?' Billy hissed. 'D'you not know

when to stand up or sit down?'

James shook his head. 'This is different to the church me and my father go to.'

Billy rolled his eyes. 'Well, just do what *I* do.'

The Mass went by in a blur, as James followed Billy's example; standing up, sitting back down, and sometimes dropping to his knees. But when the congregation began to say *The Lord's Prayer,* he smiled. This, at least, he knew.

He joined in with great gusto, glad to be able to take part. But, as the rest of the congregation fell silent, James still spoke out.

'For thine is the kingdom... *oof!*' he gasped, as Billy pulled him back down to his seat.

A whisper of stifled giggles rose from the children seated beside them.

'We don't *do* that bit!' Billy hissed. 'Now listen, everyone from our class is away to go up for communion, but you *can't*. You *have* to stay here.'

'Why?'

'Because you're not a Catholic! You just can't!'

James sat back and watched, still confused, as the pews emptied, and long lines of people walked to the front of the church. A gentle song began, and he snuggled into himself, as the quiet atmosphere, the soft light from the stained-glass windows and the low drone of the priest's voice—all lent themselves to a growing warmth.

Then, he almost cried out in surprise, his mind in a

whirl, as Billy grabbed him by the collar and hauled him to his feet.

'Look like you're singing,' Billy spoke from the side of his mouth. 'If Old McDonald knows you were sleeping, you'll get belted!'

James hardly heard his cousin's words but managed to stay upright and open and close his mouth at almost the correct times.

'I fell asleep,' he whispered, hardly aware of what he was saying.

'No kidding! I thought you were going to start snoring!'

The hymn ended, and the congregation remained on their feet as the priest gave a final blessing and then said, 'The Mass has ended. Go in peace.'

The organ began a slow, sombre tune, and the pupils and teachers stood in silence, allowing the grieving families to leave first. Then, row by row, the children were led outside.

Somewhere, a clock tower started to chime. As the third hour struck, St Mary's bells began to ring. A second later the air came alive with the pealing of bells, as every church within hearing distance added their own to the throng.

'I like this,' James said. 'This is good.'

'Aye,' Billy agreed. 'It's still sad, but it's… nice.'

'Hiya,' a small voice came from behind them. They

turned to find Ben standing there, dressed in his best clothes, his eyes red from weeping.

'Hey, Ben.' Billy said.

'Are you all right?' James asked.

Ben's mouth quivered as he nodded. But before more tears could fall, his mother and Charlotte came to his side.

'Hello, boys,' Mrs Wilson said, as Charlotte hugged them both. 'Ben'll be off school for another couple o' days. It might be best no' tae come and ask him out t'play either, eh?'

Before they could reply, Mrs Wilson took her children's hands and led them down the lane, weaving in and out of the crowd which headed back into Lochee.

'You were right,' Billy said.

'Hmm?'

'About Charlotte. You were right,' Billy repeated, his voice low, soft and a little sad. 'I *do* like her.'

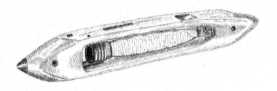

21

JAMES AND BILLY

Ben's front door remained closed for the rest of that week. The boys decided that it would be wrong to go to the den without him—although Kevin convinced them to make one *quick* visit, to clear out the awful stone wool.

Friday morning came, and although Lochee had little to celebrate, St Mary's school had been closed, as Lord Baden Powell visited Dundee.

Billy lay sleeping, having snuck back to bed. But Lily had grabbed James after breakfast and forced him to play with her and her rag dolls. They both sat on the living room floor as Lily, lost in her own little world, poured invisible cups of tea from invisible teapots, for the vaguely human-shaped scraps of material and a slightly blushing James.

'Boys! Shoes on!' With no warning, Uncle Wullie's voice boomed around the house.

James jumped up. 'Sorry, Lily!' he called, and escaped into the bedroom.

'What? Huh?' A sleepy-eyed Billy scratched his head.

'Uncle Wullie says we have to get our shoes on,' James replied, hurrying to tie his laces.

'Ohhh…!' Billy gave a long moan and sat up.

'Are you boys ready, then?' Mr Harkins appeared at the bedroom door. 'Shoes on? Hair brushed?'

'Well, my shoes are nearly on,' Billy said, his hair looking like a nest which even rats would shun.

'Good enough,' his father replied. 'Let's go then.'

The boys glanced at each other. *Go? Go Where?*

They had no idea but hurried after Mr Harkins as he turned and left the house.

♯ ♯ ♯

Ten minutes later, the boys stood on the main weaving flat of Camperdown Works. The thunderous crashing and thumping of the huge looms assaulted their ears.

As Uncle Wullie led them through a maze of people and machines, James walked in a daze. The constant *thump-thump-thump* of the machines filled his head, while Billy stared at the goings-on with great interest, shouting questions as they went.

Jute dust hung in the air; it caked the windows which ran the length of the huge space, and coated the floors, the machines and the wood and metal beams in the roof.

As well as the mass of men and women, small boys and girls moved back and forth constantly, carrying bundles of jute cloth, thick spools of twine, and large bobbins of thread. James watched in amazement as others crawled underneath the thundering looms to extract broken pieces of wood and empty thread spools—or leaned dangerously over the clattering machines to remove scraps of fabric from a web of dangling threads.

James shuddered. He had never had a reason to try and imagine what the inside of a mill was like. But he never would have believed it was like this. It was as if the entire building was a noisy, powerful animal— demanding that the tiny humans kept it fed.

As Uncle Wullie led the boys back out of the main gate, James's head throbbed in time with the machines.

After the clamour of the mill, the house seemed an oasis of silence. James joined Alice—who was darning some socks in the living room—as Billy and his parents spoke in the kitchen.

'What did *you* make of the mill, James?' Alice asked.

'I don't know,' he replied. 'There was so much going on, and it was so noisy and dusty. I felt a bit dizzy.'

Alice nodded. 'Yes, and it never changes,' she said. 'I was *so* very lucky to end up where I am. It isn't nearly as bad upstairs.'

'Is it true you get paid more than some other workers?'

Alice smiled. 'Well, not *yet*. But I will, once my training's finished. It feels a bit odd, though. I'll be making more than *Dad* does. But it'll be good to be able to help out. That's what they're talking to Billy about.'

'What? Are they making him go to work in the mills?' James asked.

'No, no. They're just asking him what he thought about it. And if he wants to, he could do what they call *half-time work*, after school.'

'Oh,' James said. Then his brow furrowed. 'Why aren't they asking me?'

'Oh, I don't think you're going to end up working in the *mills*. Do you, James?'

Before he could reply, there was a knock at the front door, and a moment later Aunt June's voice rang through the house.

'Billy, James… there's someone at the door for ye!' she called.

James ran from the sitting room, almost crashing into Billy, as his cousin dashed from the kitchen and flung the front door wide.

Ben and Charlotte stood on the pletty.

'Ben!' They called out together, their faces a mixture of shock and delight.

'Hi,' Ben said, grinning. 'Are you coming out?'

'Aye! Hang on a minute,' Billy said, then turned and called into the house. 'Mum! Can me and James...'

'Of course ye can,' she replied, before Billy had finished. 'Away ye go and play. It'll get ye out from under my feet!'

The boys bounded out onto the pletty.

'Ben... Charlotte... how are you? It's been *ages*! How is everything? Are you all right?' James and Billy jabbered, their voices overlapping.

'We're as well as can be expected,' Charlotte gave a small, sad, smile. 'It's difficult, though.'

'I thought you'd be away to the Magdalen Green today, for the big scout thing?' Billy said to Ben.

'Mum said it would be too busy and noisy for me. I don't mind missing it,' Ben replied.

'And anyway,' Charlotte brightened a little. 'What about this den of yours?'

The boys' mouths dropped open. Billy glared at Ben, who had taken a sudden interest in the ground at his feet.

'What about the den?' Billy said, through lightly gritted teeth.

'Andrew told me it's really nice.'

'Aye... aye, it is...'

'And he told me about the stone wool!' Charlotte laughed. 'You sillies, you should have known about that.' She paused for a second. 'So, can I come and see it?'

'But... but we swore...' Billy said. 'We... well...'

'I know what happened,' Charlotte said. 'But, as I

said to Andrew, I'm his *sister*. So, if you're all his *blood brothers*, then I must be in there *somewhere*, no?'

James and Billy glanced at each other, unable to think of any argument against Charlotte's point. Eventually, Billy shrugged and said, 'Fair enough.'

Charlotte clapped her hands, then turned and ran back to her house.

'Where's she going?' Ben said.

'*I* don't know! She's *your* sister!' said Billy. 'But what's going on, Ben? How come Charlotte's here? She's *far* too old to be bothering with dens!'

'Ach, my mum said I had to get out of the house,' Ben grumped. 'She told Charlotte to come with me to the den, and make sure I was all right.'

'Hmmm,' Billy said.

Charlotte soon re-appeared and almost skipped back to the boys.

'Here!' she thrust a bundle at Billy.

'What is it?' he asked.

'Some old blankets. I thought you might need some, what with the stone wool…' Charlotte smiled, and James couldn't help but notice Billy mirroring her smile.

As they set off, Charlotte chatted about how things had been for her since she left school. She spoke about something called the *Land Girls* and mentioned how their brother, Henry, was working more and more hours since their father had died.

When they reached the den, the boys spread the blankets over the linoleum floor. Once they were settled, Charlotte dipped into the wide pocket at the front of her pinafore and drew out the last thing the boys could have expected.

'COMICS!' they yelled together.

They snatched at the folded sheets of brightly coloured paper and lay them over the floor.

'Look, there's *The Funny Wonder*, two *Lot-o'-Fun*, two *Chips*...'

'Are there any of *The Rainbow*?' Ben asked.

'Three!' Charlotte replied.

She sat back and watched as the boys began to read aloud to each other. But even as they were reading, James noticed that Billy kept sneaking glances at Charlotte from behind the large pages.

After a while, Charlotte stretched out her arms. 'Well, boys,' she said. 'It's been very nice seeing your den. I hope you have a lot of fun with it. But we should probably head back, Andrew. Mum will be expecting us for dinner.'

Ben sighed and put down his comic. 'All right. I'll see you two later, aye? I'll ask my mum if I can come back after dinner.' Ben shifted the roof to the side, and James and Billy clambered out to wave the Wilsons off as they made their way down the hill.

'What shall we do now?' James said. 'We could go to the building site? Or will we just go home?'

'Hmmm... I dunno,' Billy said, pointing upward.

James squinted at the sky. Mountainous grey clouds had gathered in the east. A chill wind picked up and whipped the long grass against the boys' legs.

'I think it's going to...'

With a flash of lightning, the heavens opened, and rain drove down in sheets. Billy yelled and dived towards the den. He threw himself flat on his belly, sliding down through the entrance. James, shrieking as loud as his cousin, followed on Billy's heels and almost landed on top of him, as he slithered in.

'The roof!' Billy cried.

'But it's made of metal!' James called back.

'Just get it over us! We'll be fine!'

They dragged the metal sheet forward, then collapsed to the floor of the den, drenched and gasping for breath. Heavy rain drummed onto the canvas-clad roof.

'Poor Ben and Charlotte. They'll be caught in that!' James said.

'Rather them than us!' Billy grinned and retrieved Kevin's matchbox. He lit a waiting fire-pot, as James nervously inched the iron sheet back.

The heat from the fire soon warmed the den, making the air almost stifling. Steam rose from the boys, as their clothes began to dry.

'Do you think they'll be gone soon?' James said.

'Who?' Billy's eyes were half closed.

'The builders.'

Billy yawned. 'Well, there can't be *too* much left for them to do.'

'I hope they don't take everything away in this direction. They might find the den.'

'Nah, all the cart-tracks run up towards the Gelly burn. They've probably come from Ardler Woods, or maybe Americanmuir. It's probably why they haven't bothered us.'

There was a low rumble of distant thunder, and the silence lengthened as the boys listened to the muffled beat of the rain.

'I wonder how long it will be before the war ends,' James said.

Billy made no reply.

'Billy?' A soft snore told James all he needed to know.

He rolled onto his side and allowed his eyelids to droop. The heat from the fire, and the steady, lulling sound of the rain, surrounded James as if he were wrapped in soft woollen blankets.

He felt sleep trying to fall on top of him; he didn't fight it.

22

THE HOUSE

The rain soaked into the hole, making the ground slick with mud. James stood and gazed over a grassland which was scarred with shell-holes, to a broad horizon, broken by tangled barbed wire fences.

The sides of the den snaked off into the distance, cutting a winding trench into the countryside. Some soldiers stood, rifles to their shoulders, as another man washed his face in a small bird-patterned bowl.

'They Jerries'll get battered if they even think of trying to wreck this.' Billy said, adjusting his tarnished metal helmet, and fixing a bayonet to his rifle.

An explosion shook the ground. James cowered, as clods of mud and tattered comic pages blasted into the sky. Men began shouting, making no sense. Some ran over the top of the trench. Some fell and lay still.

From far off, the voice of James's father called out to

him—but was drowned out by a harsh rattling noise: a Vickers machine gun had opened fire. He couldn't see it, but the rattling continued to hammer through him, like the sound of rain on a tin roof...

✠ ✠ ✠

The den roof rattled, as Kevin and Derek and Ben dragged the iron sheet sideways.

'Daddy!' James cried aloud.

'What?' said Kevin.

James blinked, and wiped his face with his hand. 'Nothing... I think I was dreaming,' he mumbled.

The three boys jumped into the den, leaving the roof aside. The rain had passed, and the sky was again a brilliant blue.

'Ben? I thought you had to go home?' James said.

'That was *ages* ago! How long've you been sleeping?'

'We've brought presents!' Derek announced, as he and Kevin dropped bundles to the floor.

'Huh?' Billy woke up with a start. 'What is it?'

'Wake up!' Kevin yelled. 'We've brought cushions!'

'Cushions?'

'Aye! We *liberated* them from Auld Kelbie's cart.'

James gaped. 'You *stole* them?'

'Nah, we just... helped them fall off. Then the Raggie went away, and they were still lying on the ground. It wasn't *our* fault he didn't see them,' Derek chipped in.

'I don't care,' Billy mumped. 'Ye've let all the heat out.'

Ben was given the honour of re-lighting the fire. Once the flames had taken hold, the boys sprawled on the blanketed floor, heads supported by stolen cushions. They spoke about McLintock, about the building site, and wondered what the new building might be.

'What's *your* house like, James? Is it like Camperdown House?' Ben asked.

James laughed. 'No, not at all. It's just a house.'

'But it's bigger than mine, though.'

'Well, yes, I suppose it is.'

'Have you got servants?' Derek piped up.

'Servants? No, but there's Mary and Toosh. They're the housekeepers.'

'You've got servants!' Billy mocked.

'No, really, they're just... I don't know... they look after the house and me and my father...' James's mouth dried up. A light shiver ran through him as a memory resurfaced of Mary and Toosh, standing by his side, as the shiny, black car drove his father away.

'It sounds nice,' Ben said.

'Yes... it is.' James eventually said. 'Maybe you could come and visit when my father comes home?'

Billy snorted. 'Ha! Don't think so. Can you see *housekeepers* letting us lot into a bonny, clean house?'

James spread his arms wide, showing off his rough

clothes. 'Oh, I don't know, look at me!'

'And me!' said Derek.

'Me too!' said Ben.

'But that's what's so good about this den,' Kevin said. 'You don't need to be dressed nice to come into it. I mean... I don't own anything that *is* nice.'

The boys laughed again, but James fell silent. He'd never thought of his friends as *poor*, but he couldn't deny they were the closest thing to it that he had ever known.

'I wish...' he began.

'What?' Billy asked. 'What is it?'

'Oh, I don't know... I just wish we could all go and live in my house.'

'Ha! I can just *see* your housekeepers' faces!' Derek laughed. '*Oh no—the carpets! Oh no—the couch! Oh no—the solid gold toilet!*'

James smiled, but his time living with the Harkins had made him realise how much of his *own* house lay unused, and, although he ached to be back home, he suddenly thought it might seem a little cold and lonely when he returned.

'When I leave school, I'm going to get a *huge* house right up here,' said Kevin.

'Leave? We've just started Primary Six!' said Billy

'Aye, I know. But next year we'll be in Primary Seven!'

'Not if you start half-time at the mill!'

'Aye. We'll be the *big boys* then,' Derek grinned. 'No

more being called "all you small boys" by everyone. We'll rule the whole school!'

'But it's a whole year away,' James said. 'You might not even end up in the same class.'

'I'm pretty sure it'll be Mr Ferguson's,' Billy replied.

'What?'

'Next year, in Primary Seven. We'll probably be in Mr Ferguson's class.'

'What? *Mad Jock*?' Ben asked.

'Which one is he again?' James asked.

'He's the really tall teacher,' Billy explained. 'He does history and art. He's a bit baldy, with a wee white beard. He looks like… thingmy… that actor… from that film…'

The others chuckled at Billy's description.

'Does he look like… that man… from that shop?' Kevin giggled.

'Or that guy… from that football team?' Derek added.

Billy threw evil looks at his friends, as they laughed.

'Anyway, what about *you*, James?' Ben asked all at once. 'You might not even *be* here next year.'

'Aye,' Billy grinned wickedly. 'And you'd miss Teeny Robbins, wouldn't you?'

A fiery blush bloomed on James's face. He cursed himself for having asked Billy the name of the girl who sat by the classroom door, next to Finlay.

'James loooves her sooo much! Almost as much as he loves *school*!' Billy cooed.

'I didn't say that,' James said. 'And anyway, you…'

He almost bit his tongue, as he snapped his mouth closed to stop himself from throwing Billy's liking of Charlotte back at him. He didn't want to make Ben feel awkward. All he could do was sit, red-faced, and make half-hearted denials about Teeny Robbins, which only made the others tease him all the more.

The truth was, he hardly knew her—but he *did* like her. She was a clever, pretty girl, who was always one of the first to raise her hand, whenever Mr Marra asked questions of the class.

'I wish *I* could go to another school,' Ben said. 'Or maybe go to Edinburgh with Charlotte.'

Billy sat up, his mocking of James forgotten.

'What do you mean, Ben?' he asked.

'Charlotte,' Ben replied. 'She's going to Edinburgh at the end of the week. She applied to be a *Land Girl*, and got a letter yesterday saying she's been accepted.'

'Umm… What's a Land Girl?' Kevin asked.

Ben sighed. 'A Land Girl…' he intoned—like someone who has listened to the same speech over and over again and is very bored of hearing it—'…is a young lady, aged eighteen or over, who will work the land while our brave boys are fighting the enemy abroad. These plucky lasses will do the jobs our bold boys cannot. Blah, blah, blah.'

His voice changed back to normal. 'It goes on and on like that for ages. All it means, is that she's going to work on a farm.' He slumped down on his cushion. 'It's all I've been hearing for the last month. Can we maybe talk about something else?'

Derek threw his cushion at Ben, who threw his back, missed, and hit Kevin. In a matter of seconds, cushions were flying about the cramped space. They bounced off the walls, the roof, and heads and bodies—and narrowly missed the flaming paint pot.

In the middle of the shouts and yells Billy sat staring at the floor, giving no reaction, even when a cushion thumped into his chest. Suddenly, he spun round and scrabbled through the den's entrance.

'Hey! Where're ye going?' Derek called at Billy's back.

'I'm going to see if there's anything good at the building site.'

'Are you daft? It's soaking out there!'

'I'm going to go and have a look too,' James said.

'Nah, you're not escaping!' Kevin swung a cushion.

James ducked, and wrestled his way out of the den. Ben, Kevin and Derek howled with laughter as they beat their cushions upon his back and legs. But James wasn't laughing. He'd seen the way Billy's face had fallen, when Ben spoke about Charlotte leaving Lochee. He ran through the damp grass until he reached the nearly-completed building and scrabbled through an open window. James dropped into a large, vacant space. He stood for a moment, staring at the bare stone walls in the dim room. Despite the sun outside, the windows were too filthy to let much light in.

James's heart sank as a familiar sound reached him. He ran up the concrete stairs, two at a time, and popped his head into the first room he found. There, huddled in a corner, arms crossed over his knees, and face buried in his sleeves, sat Billy, weeping.

'Hey, Billy,' James said.

'Go away.' Billy's voice sounded muffled through his sleeves. 'Leave me alone.'

'Aw, Billy. It's not like she's going away forever.'

Billy lifted his head, his eyes were red and bleary. 'You don't *know* that,' he yelled. 'She might *never* come back! She's going to Edinburgh. That's nearly a hundred miles away, and it's all posh and huge. Why would she ever want to come back to Lochee after being there?' Billy dropped his head to his arms, as his tears came again.

James sat on the cold stone floor and draped an arm across Billy's shoulders, as his cousin poured out his heart in heavy sobs. After a while, Billy's breath stopped hitching.

'You all right?' James ventured.

'Yes,' Billy sniffed, and nodded.

'Do you want to go back to the den?'

Billy wiped his face on his sleeve. 'Do you think the others will know I've been crying?'

James studied Billy's face; pink streaks lined his

cheeks, where his tears had washed away the grime and dirt. James couldn't help himself. He burst out laughing.

'Thanks a *lot*!' Billy said, and shoved at his cousin.

James fell sideways. 'Oh... oh, my sides,' he said, as cramp hit him. 'Oh, Billy... you... your face!'

'Fine, so it was a stupid question!' Billy tried to be angry, but James's laughter came even harder and Billy couldn't help but laugh along with him.

As their giggling died away, Billy sprang upright.

'Hey!' he said. 'I bet we're the first people to be in this house, now that it's finished.'

'Yes, we probably are,' James agreed.

Without another word, Billy rushed out of the door. James was so shocked that it took him a moment to react and follow his cousin. He reached the top of the stairway and called down.

'Billy!'

No reply came back. James took a step down, but then a door opened behind him.

'I bet I'm the first person to do *that* in this house!' Billy announced, grinning, as he buttoned up his trousers. The toilet bowl could be heard filling up in the bathroom. 'I've never had a wee in an indoor toilet before. Lucky the water is working though, eh?'

'But... oh... yes, the flush,' James said. 'But I didn't hear you running the tap to wash your hands?'

'Who said I *did*?' Billy's wicked grin slid back into

place. Then he rubbed his hands all over his cousin's head. 'Ewwww! Germs! Disease!'

'Euuurggh!' James recoiled in absolute horror as Billy fled downstairs.

James leapt after him. The boys chased through the house, until James cornered Billy in the room with the open window. He lunged at his cousin, catching Billy's foot as he tried to climb back outside. Billy tumbled, as James scrambled out and thumped down beside him.

'You're *horrible!*' James said, thumping Billy's arm.

'Maybe I am,' Billy grinned. 'But at least I don't have wee all over my head!'

James threw himself at his cousin and the two boys wrestled, rolling over and over in the drying mud.

'Hey! What're you laddies up to?' A deep, angry voice broke over their squeals of mock pain and outrage.

'The watchie!' Billy hissed. 'Come on!' He pulled James to his feet and began to run.

'We… we're going the wrong way!' James gasped, breathless in his efforts to keep up.

'Doesn't… matter…' Billy panted, slamming his feet into the ground as fast as he could. 'Follow me!'

'Get back here you two!' The harsh voice shouted again. 'I'll get the Polis on tae the pair o' ye!'

The boys ran even faster, barging through the long, wet grass, flying across the muddy ground.

Just as James's strength began to fail—Billy hit the

ground. James collapsed beside him, his legs slick with wet grass and mud splatters.

'Who was that?' James said gasping for breath.

'The watchie,' Billy wheezed. 'A *watchman*. They look after building sites.'

'Is he still after us?'

'I don't know... I don't *hear* him.'

The cousins kept still, catching their breath and listening for any sound of pursuit. Nothing but distant birdsong could be heard. Slowly, they crouched and peered over the top of the long grass. The coast was clear.

'That was close,' Billy said. 'Can you imagine trying to explain *that* one to my mum? I can just hear her. "*You'll get sent tae The Mars, William Harkins!*"'

James smiled; Billy's impression was perfect.

⚜ ⚜ ⚜

They had only walked for a few minutes, when a sharp and sudden burst of laughter rose from the ground behind them. They chuckled in amused amazement— they had passed the den without even noticing it.

Turning round, they squirmed into the den's entrance.

'Have you been crying?' Kevin immediately asked.

Billy squared his shoulders. 'No! What would I have been crying for?'

'Look at the state of you! Were you two fighting?'

'No, we were chased by the watchman. Billy fell over and got winded.' James said quickly.

'*Anyway...*' Ben said, rolling his eyes, '...I was just saying to Derek and Kevin, we've got a half-day on Friday, so maybe we could all go down to see Charlotte off at the station?'

'Where's the train leaving from?' Derek asked.

'The Tay Bridge Station, at quarter past three.'

The boys fell into a conversation about trains, and school on Monday, and odd days off. They all agreed that they would try to make it to the station for Charlotte's big send-off, then pushed the roof wide, to watch the sun fall towards the Tay.

The ground was almost dry, and Kevin suggested they play a few rounds of *Dead Man's Fall*. The boys yelled and screamed, as they were machine gunned, blown up, and occasionally bayonetted. Their shouts and cries flew over the swaying, yellow sea, until—after dying many deaths, in a thousand gruesome ways—they became too tired to do anything else but sit down.

They rested on a small hump in the grass, just high enough to see the horizon, where the sun caught the river in the west. None of them spoke, but after a while James became aware that Kevin had started humming to himself. The others didn't seem to notice. Then the humming stopped, and Kevin began to sing, under his breath, still staring off into the distance:

'...*and The God of All Small Boys... is looking down ...is looking dowwwn ...on meeee...*' he sang gently, a shadow of a smile on his lips.

Billy, Derek and Ben joined in, their voices as low as Kevin's, repeating the phrase he had just sung. James was a heartbeat away from asking what they were singing, when Kevin spoke.

'These are the best days,' he said.

'What?' Derek gasped. 'Are you daft? We've got to go back to school on Monday!'

'No, really, they are,' said Kevin. 'I mean, we've had a good laugh, the den's *brilliant*, there's no more workmen about, and the whole place is *ours* now. I told you before—*The God of All Small Boys* really *is* looking out for us.

'Life is just one, big, jammy piece!'

The others stared at Kevin for a second, then they all burst out laughing.

23

TEENY ROBBINS

As the boys reached the top of Bright Street, Kevin stopped suddenly.

'Look!' he pointed upwards. 'I love seeing the moon when the sun's still out.'

They stood for a moment, staring into the dark blue sky. The ghost of an almost full moon hung above them.

'Do ye think people'll ever *go* to the moon?' said Ben.

'I saw a movie at the *Empire*, about men who went to the moon,' Billy said. 'I don't remember a lot about it though; I was only wee. You could see all the stars and planets, and they...'

'Where have you lot been, then?' a voice interrupted.

The boys turned in all directions, looking for the owner of the voice.

'Hey! Up here!' It came again. 'I see ye, Billy Harkins. And you, James Gunning!'

The boys tilted their heads. At the top of the nearest close, a net curtain flapped in the evening breeze, and a face peeped out of the wide-open window.

'Hurrah! The clever laddies find a window!'

'Shut up, Teeny! Away and play with your dollies!'

The girl's face creased in mock anger.

'Dollies? I'll give ye dollies, Billy Harkins!' She ducked down from the window, then reappeared. 'Dollies, is it?' she cried, and began hurling something at the boys.

'Ow,' Derek exclaimed, as one of the objects smacked into his elbow. 'What *is* that?'

'Ooya!' Another *something* bounced off Kevin's neck.

The boys ducked, crossing their arms over their heads as they tried to avoid the tiny missiles. Then the attack stopped, as quickly as it had begun. The pavement around the boys' feet was dotted with horse chestnuts.

'Conkers?' Derek said.

'Hey!' Billy called up to the window. 'How come you just happen to have a pile of wee conkers ready to throw at people? Are ye daft?'

'No,' the girl replied. 'We're savin' them for the war. Ye can get money for them. Where've ye all been, anyway? You lot don't live up the Tofthill!'

'We were out *looking* for conkers,' James blurted out. 'But we were chased away from Camperdown.'

The others kept quiet, letting James spin his tale.

The dark-haired girl crossed her arms to lean on the

window frame. 'Ye'll no' get any at the Estate, or in the Deer Park. I was up there yesterday and most o' the trees have only got wee tottie conkers just now.'

'Umm... Yes, Billy told me that, but I've never been chestnut hunting before, so I wanted to go.'

Teeny gave James a long, hard stare.

James could do nothing but look back at her. The silence lengthened, then James blushed as Teeny gave him the tiniest of smiles.

'Anyway,' Billy broke in. 'We've got to get back home.'

'Fair enough, then,' Teeny called back, still staring at James. 'Maybe I'll see ye at school. Cheerio!'

The window closed, and she was gone.

'That was...'

'Aye, *Teeny* Robbins,' said Ben. 'Her big sister's Charlotte's pal, I think she's going to the Land Girls too.'

'Oh, yes... Christina.' James said, almost to himself.

And that was enough for the boys to torment him all the way back to the tenement.

It was also enough for Billy to insist upon telling the entire household that evening that, "*James has a lass!*"

James kept quiet, hoping it would make the teasing stop a little sooner, but mostly because he knew Billy's words were not *entirely* un-truthful.

He'd never met Teeny before, but he *did* like her.

24

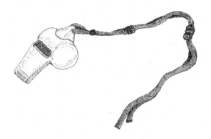

THE STATION

August slipped into September, as the weekend passed.

On Monday morning, over breakfast, Aunt June spoke to Billy and James.

'So, I think you two are both big and ugly enough tae get yerselves tae school, from now on, aye?' she said. 'And ye can look after Lily as well.'

James's heart leapt. If they were to be taking Lily home, that meant he and Billy would have to wait for her by the Girls' Gate, and *that* meant a chance to *accidentally* bump into Teeny Robbins.

'What are you smiling at?' Billy asked.

'Nothing,' James replied.

But James's hopes appeared to be dashed as the week passed. He only ever caught brief glimpses of Teeny, as she walked up the road, far ahead of them. Until, on Thursday afternoon, Lily emerged from school with

Teeny walking beside her. The two girls were lost in conversation, taking no notice of anyone around them.

James's face flushed in a deep blush. He could see Billy smiling at his embarrassment, but his cousin said nothing—until Lily walked right into him.

'Watch it!' Billy yelled, as Lily bounced off her brother.

'Ow!' Lily complained. 'What are you doing, standing where I'm wanting to walk?'

'Oh, hey,' Teeny said. 'It's *Conker Boy* and his daft pal!' She nodded at Billy but smiled broadly at James. 'You laddies must think I'm no' wise, eh?' She narrowed her eyes. 'It must be an awful good den ye've got, for ye to be tellin' lies about where ye'd been!'

Both boys stared in horror—Teeny knew about the den.

Billy rounded on Lily. 'What've you been saying?' he whispered angrily.

'What?' Lily said, a picture of innocence. 'Me and Teeny were just talking, and she said she saw you lot walking down her street. I just said you must've been away at your den.'

'How do *you* know about the den?'

Lily rolled her eyes. 'Because it's all you two talk about - the whole *house* knows about it.'

'But we never talk about where it *is*!'

'I didn't say I knew where it *was*,' Lily sighed. 'I just said I knew you *had* one.'

James and Billy sucked in deep breaths and blew them out again.

'Well, that's all right then,' Billy said. 'Come on, let's get going.'

As the four children reached High Street, Teeny turned off.

'Well, I'll see ye later,' she said.

James watched her go, until Billy dug his elbow into his cousin's ribs.

'Ow!' said James. 'What was that for?'

Billy grinned back at him. 'I thought toffs like you walked *ladies* home?'

'What?'

'Look, she's walking really slowly. She couldn't be *more* waiting for you to walk her home if she turned round and shouted at you to do it!'

'Do you think so? Really?'

'Will you just go?' Billy gave James a push.

James strode after the little dark-haired girl without saying another word.

As he came within a few feet of Teeny, he slowed down, his courage slipping away with every step. He'd never thought of having a girl for a friend before. He had no idea what to say or do, didn't know if he had the nerve to speak, or tap Teeny on the shoulder—he didn't even know if he *should* do any of those things.

'Well, you took your time, eh?' Teeny spoke, without

turning around.

James blinked, startled. *How did she know I was here?*

Teeny turned and regarded James. 'My, look at you! A right, wee gentleman, so ye are!'

'Umm... I, umm... '

'Oh, it's fine,' Teeny said. 'I just thought, maybe ye were wantin' to walk me up the road?'

'Aye. I mean... Yes.'

'Well, I cannae see anybody stoppin' ye,' Teeny smiled again, and resumed her walk. James hurried to fall into step beside her and they walked along in silence. It seemed like no time at all before they stood outside Teeny's home.

'So, are ye going to tell me about this den o' yours, then?' She asked.

'Oh... the den?' James was still a little confused. Having managed to walk Teeny home, he didn't know what to do next. He'd *expected* her to simply go into her house, but it seemed she wanted to chat.

'Well... I... I can't really talk about it,' he mumbled. 'It's sort of a secret.'

'Och, you laddies and yer big secrets!' Teeny giggled. 'There's no' much that's secret about a couple o' bits o' wood held together wi' string, is there?'

James smiled, amused at how far from the truth Teeny's description of the den was.

'So, when am I gettin' tae *see* it?' she asked.

James's face dropped again.

'Well… it isn't really up to me. I don't know if…'

Teeny laughed again. 'Och, it's *far* too easy t'get ye all embarrassed, James Gunning! Dinnae worry, I know… it's all a big secret!' She lifted her voice higher and spoke in a tremulous tone. 'Oooo, the den… the den! Nobody's allowed tae know where it is!'

James blushed even deeper. Yet, even though Teeny was making fun of him and his friends, she did it with such a smile on her face, and a glint in her eye, that he found himself liking her more and more.

'Right,' she announced. 'I'm away in. I'm goin' tae the station with my big sister tomorrow. She's away tae join the Land Girls.'

'Oh. Some of us are going there too, to see off Charlotte Wilson.'

'Och, aye! She's pals wi' my sister. Well, maybe I'll see ye there, then? Cheerio.' Teeny skipped into the building before James could say his own goodbyes.

He walked back down Bright Street in a daze. Billy and Lily still stood where he had left them. Both had wide grins on their faces. As James approached, Lily skipped around him clapping her hands and chanting, 'James is going with Tee-ny… James is going with Tee-ny!'

'I'm doing *what*?'

'You and Teeny!' Billy said. 'Is that you two Lad and

Lass now?'

'*What*? I only walked her to her house!'

'Aw, did you not give her a kiss?' Lily asked, her disappointment plain.

James and Billy's mouths fell into huge 'O' shapes—James's in shock, and Billy's in disgust.

'Ewwww,' Billy squealed. 'You *didn't*, did you?'

'No.' James could hardly speak. Walking a girl home was one thing. But *kissing* one? The thought hadn't even crossed his mind.

'Not even a wee peck on the cheek?' Lily asked.

'*No!*'

Lily shrugged. 'She probably wouldn't have let you, anyway. Y'know that boy Finlay, in your class? He tried to give her a kiss at the Easter Parade, and she punched him-really hard!'

'Well, *I* didn't!' James said.

'So, what were you talking about?' Billy asked, as they walked home.

'Nothing really,' James hesitated. 'She asked to see the den, though.'

'She did *what*?' Billy jolted to a halt.

'I didn't say she *could* But she's going to be at the station tomorrow. Her sister's going to Edinburgh with Charlotte.'

'Ach, it doesn't matter,' Billy said. 'The station'll be totally packed, you probably won't even see her.'

✦ ✦ ✦

On Friday afternoon Billy and James met the Wilsons on their shared pletty and set off for the station. They arrived just as the Auld Steeple's clock began to ring out the hour. Their timing was excellent as, when the third toll of the bells faded away, a sudden flood of soldiers came pouring onto the platform.

Billy's prediction had been correct; the station was indeed packed.

Every one of the men was dressed for war: kilted, jacketed, and wearing Glengarry bonnets which proudly displayed the Black Watch crest. Every soldier carried a satchel and a large kit-bag, and had a rifle slung over his shoulder. They arranged themselves along the platform in a perfect line, unmoving, as they waited for the train.

'Look, they're from the Black Watch. They might be going to join my father,' James whispered.

'Wow! I didn't know they'd get on the train with their guns,' Billy replied, hypnotised by the rifles.

James hardly heard him, as Teeny Robbins and her family came walking down the steep platform steps.

Billy grinned. 'Oh. I see your lass has got here, then?'

'Shut up!' James hissed. But this time, he did not blush.

Charlotte ran to greet Teeny's sister, Ellen. The girls grabbed at each other, excitedly jumping in little circles.

Mrs Wilson watched her daughter. She smiled, but her eyes still showed a hint of sadness. She took Ben's hand in a firm clasp.

Teeny waved at James. James waved back, not caring a bit as Billy rolled his eyes and muttered something under his breath.

Then—with a rumble, and a billow of smoke that reeked of coal and oil—the train pulled in. As it squealed to a halt, a Black Watch officer barked an order to the line of men. A few soldiers stepped from the ranks and crossed to the train, then each one swung open a door. Another order followed, and the rest of the soldiers flowed towards the waiting carriages, calling to each other as they boarded.

'Ladies and Gents, please note that only the three rear carriages may be used by the general public. The remainder of this train is reserved for His Majesty's forces. Thank you.' A porter moved along the platform, repeating his message as he went.

Mrs Wilson gasped. 'Oh my, this really *is* happening, isn't it? Oh, my wee lassie,' she sobbed, hugging Charlotte fiercely. Ben wrapped his arms around them both, and for a moment they stood, holding each other in silence

Then a whistle sounded—sharp and clear in the steaming, hissing air—and Charlotte and Ellen squealed with excitement. Their mothers spoke a few words to them, hugging them all the while, before the girls clambered onto the train with their small suitcases.

The porter walked back along the platform, checking every door, as more smoke and steam rose from the engine. Once he reached the far end, he raised his flag and gave a long blast on his whistle.

The train gave a jerk and a shunt, then eased away from the platform. Both mothers' hands leapt to their mouths, stifling little sobs, as Charlotte and Ellen pressed their hands to the carriage window in farewell.

Billy's resolve broke. Heavy tears gathered in his eyes and silently over-spilled. As he watched the train pull away, Charlotte's eyes met his. She smiled a little, lifted her hand and blew him a kiss. Despite his tears, Billy smiled back, and waved as if his life depended on it.

Then, with a deafening roar, the train began to pick up speed. In moments it had steamed beyond the station, becoming little more than a toy in the distance.

Oily smoke hung over the silent platform. Mrs Wilson still gazed after the distant train as the Robbins began to leave. Teeny turned her tear-filled eyes towards James and gave him a sad smile, as she joined her family.

It was not until she had taken it away that James realised—she had been holding his hand all along.

25

THE STARLING

'Honest. She was holding his hand!' Billy cheerfully announced to his gathered friends.

'It wasn't me. *She* took *my* hand. I didn't know!' James protested.

'You were still holding hands! You're *so* in love!'

'Hang on though,' Kevin interrupted. 'Teeny took your hand. Is that right, James?'

James nodded, confused at Kevin's solemn question.

'And you didn't notice she had?'

'No.'

'Hmmm... That's quite serious.'

'What? Why?'

'Well, if she held your hand, and you didn't notice... I reckon the wedding will have to be next week.'

It took a second for the boys to react to Kevin's dead-pan delivery, then they broke into hysterical laughter.

'It's not *that* funny,' James huffed, stuffing his hands into his coat pocket. Something rustled. 'What's this?'

He pulled out a scrap of paper, and eager eyes watched as he unfolded it to reveal a message, written in pencil, in neat, precise handwriting.

I like you, James Gunning, it read—the '*i*' of '*like*' was dotted with a tiny heart.

The boys' laughter exploded again, as James blushed to shame the sun.

'Billy was bubbling when Charlotte got on the train!' he shouted, desperate to change the subject.

'Doesn't matter! *I* never got a *love letter* from anyone!' Billy yelled, and the laughter grew louder.

James slumped against the wall, as Kevin stood Billy and Ben side-by-side. 'Bride here, Groom here, please!'

'Ooh! A wedding!' Derek clapped, as the *Bride* and *Groom* tried to keep their faces straight.

'Dearly beloved,' said Kevin. 'We are gathered here today to ask *The God of All Small Boys* to...'

'We ken whaur yer den is!'

The boys' laughter washed away, as if a bucket of ice water had been thrown over them. They turned, to find John McLintock leaning against a lamp-post, his hands stuffed in his pockets. Two of his gang stood by his side, shuffling nervously from foot to foot.

'Did ye no' hear me?' he smirked. 'I said—we ken whaur yer den is.'

'You do *not*!' Billy's hands curled into fists.

'Aye, we do,' McLintock replied, looking at the sky and grinning a grin that James wanted to punch. '...and we're gonnae totally *wreck* it.'

'No... you don't.' James reasoned. 'If you knew where it was you wouldn't have told us. You would've just wrecked it, and then waited for us to find it.'

'Oh, d'ye think so, *posh laddie*? Well, we'll just have tae see, won't we?'

'So where is it then?' James asked, surprising himself at how brave he sounded.

McLintock laughed. 'Oh no. I'm no' sayin' anythin'. If ye dinnae want tae believe me, then that's your problem. But I'm tellin' ye,' He pushed himself from the lamp-post and jabbed a finger towards Billy. 'We *ken* whaur it is— and it's gonnae get *wrecked*!'

McLintock swaggered away; his minions scurried after him.

For a moment, Billy and his friends watched them go. Then, as if someone had burst a paper bag behind them, they jumped into a huddle and began talking all at once—frantic in their shared anger, disbelief, and worry.

'So, what're we going to do?' Derek asked. 'We can't ignore it. He *might* actually know.'

'Wait a minute,' said Kevin. 'It's not like he's going to be able to wreck it at night, is he?'

'Eh? Why wouldn't he?' Ben asked.

'Because it'd be too dark, for a start. Even *we* wouldn't be able to find the den at night-time. And anyway, his mum would *batter* him if he got caught out really late at night.'

The others nodded. It was true—mothers seemed to have a terrible, illogical hatred for young, adventurous boys staying out late.

'But what's that got to do with anything?' Billy said.

'Everything!' Kevin paced as he spoke. 'Look, if McLintock *does* know where it is, he's not going to wait *forever* before he tries to wreck it, is he? So, we'll all have to try and stay at the den as long as we can... at least for the next few days.

'So, I'll nip home just now, and tell my mum I'm not really hungry, and grab a piece and jam or something, and we'll all head up to the den. Then, when you lot go home for your tea, I'll just *stay* there and eat my piece!

'Then once you've all *had* your tea, you can come back to the den, and we'll *all* stay there until it gets late.'

'But not *too* late?' Ben said, a little worried.

'No, not *too* late. Just late enough to *nearly* get into trouble. It'll be fine.'

'Right!' Billy stepped up to command his troops. 'We'll have to go right now. Kevin, away and get your piece. If McLintock *is* on his way to the den, we'll be able to see him on the road from Ma Donnelly's house. If we don't see him, we'll wait there for you.'

Kevin bolted off as the others marched up Bright Street. They quickened their pace as they reached the main road, keeping a watchful eye for anyone who might be following them as they left Lochee.

They reached a bend in the road, where a single house sat surrounded by a stone dyke.

'Good, there's no-one on the road up to Camperdown. Go round the corner,' Billy ordered, 'if we sit on the pavement no-one'll see us.'

They sat with their backs against the dyke, not daring to speak, until the sound of running feet reached them.

'James, sneak a look,' Billy hissed.

But before James could move, Kevin came pelting around the corner, almost falling over his friends.

'Did anyone follow you lot?' Kevin gasped.

'No, don't think so. But we should go the long way, though—just in case. Are you ready?' Billy asked.

'Aye, Aye. I've got my piece. Just… give me a minute.'

When Kevin had caught his breath, Billy led the pack along the far edge of the Camperdown Estate. They headed east, through Dryburgh, until they came to the Gelly burn, where they stopped downstream from a massive boulder. Billy, Derek and Kevin stooped to drink from the river, as Ben spoke to James.

'This is *The Brewery*,' he said. 'We always have a drink from here. And that wee dip in the riverbank is The Fishery—loads of sticklebacks live there. And that big boulder's The Wee Stane.'

'The Wee Stane? But it looks quite large,' said James.

'It's not called The Wee Stane because it's wee, James.'
Ben grinned.

'Come on, we have to hurry!' Billy called, before
James could ask Ben what he meant.

They trudged southwards through the long grass,
until they reached the newly-finished house. All signs of
the builders had gone. It stood, empty and alone, at the
centre of a wide patch of churned, muddy ground.

'Awh, poor house,' Ben said, as they left it behind. 'I
hope it's not empty too long.'

No answer came from the rest, as they reached the
den.

'There's no *way* that McLintock knows where this is!'
Billy spoke with certainty.

The others made small noises of agreement.

They piled into the den and began to tidy it up. They
smoothed their blankets and straightened the pile of
paint pots. But, as they were shifting cushions from one
place to another, Derek cried out.

'Aww, hey! How did this get in here?'

Lying in the join of two blankets, was a dead starling.
Derek prodded it with his foot, and a horrific stench
rose from the corpse.

'Crivvens... it stinks! How long has it *been* in here?'
Kevin complained. 'I'm not staying in here with this

rotten thing! Get it out!'

'*You* get it out,' Billy said. 'I'm not picking it up!'

'Baggsie not me!'

'Baggsie not me either!'

'Or me!'

'Derek *found* it!'

James sighed. 'Hold on,' he said, and left the den.

He returned carrying a sturdy stick which forked at the end, making a ragged 'Y' shape. He gave it to Kevin.

'Here,' he said. 'You can use this to pick it up.'

'Me?'

'You're the one who has to stay here,' James grinned.

Kevin rolled his eyes, snatched the stick from James's hand and gingerly slid it under the dead bird. He lifted it with great care and then turned to the others with a look of joyous evil on his face.

'Ewww... Disease! Disease!' he cackled, poking the stick towards them.

Shrieking like banshees, the boys threw off the roof and sprang out of the den, desperate to get away. Kevin followed, the bird still jammed in the fork of the stick.

The others scattered, glancing behind themselves, squealing and giggling, but Ben stumbled on a small hillock and fell to the ground. As he scrambled to get back up, Kevin slid the corpse down the back of his shirt.

'Eeeeewww!' Ben yelled. 'It's slimy and hoorrrible!'

His friends gathered round him, giggling even more

as Ben pulled his shirt out of his shorts. The small body dropped to the ground.

'Hey,' Billy said. 'Where's its head?'

They began to search the ground around Ben's feet but found nothing. Then Ben gave a low moan of utter disgust. 'Eeewww... It's in my paaaaants!'

The others collapsed to the ground, as Ben hopped from one foot to the other, trying to rid himself of the offending object. Eventually, the sad remains of the bird fell out of his shorts. Red-faced, and revolted beyond words, he crushed the head with the sole of his boot.

When they had all recovered, the boys wandered back to the den. They set the roof in place and lay down in the warmth of a fire-pot—until it was time for them to say their goodbyes to Kevin.

'What'll you do if McLintock comes while we're away?' James asked.

'Och, that's no problem,' Derek said. 'Kevin'll just have to batter him himself!'

'Seriously, though,' Billy said. 'If he *does* come, hit him with a pot, or something, all right?'

'I shall defend this post with my very life, *sir*!' Kevin declared, giving a bad salute.

The others grinned and heaved the roof of the den.

'Aw no!' Ben whined, squirming. 'There's feathers sticking to my bum!'

It took another ten minutes of screaming hysterics

before the rest were recovered enough to leave.

# # #

Almost an hour had passed by the time James and Billy wolfed down their tea and headed back to Bright Street. Derek joined them, as they waited for Ben. James hoped that Christina might poke her head out of the window as they waited, but she didn't.

When Ben arrived, they set off for the den. As they walked, they spoke more of their plan, but it soon became clear—if McLintock really knew where the den was, they couldn't do much to protect it.

'All he'd have to do is plunk-off school for a day, and that's it!' Derek said, as they reached the edge of the large field of yellow grass.

'But wouldn't he get into trouble?' James said.

'Pffft... as if he cares. If anybody from St Mary's is going to end up on *The Mars*, it's him. He's never... Hey... What's that?' Derek pointed across the field.

A tall pillar of thick, black smoke rose from the middle of the grassland.

Each boy's face turned white. Then they ran—faster than they ever had in their lives.

26

THE WHITE ROOM

James, Billy, Ben and Derek shivered as they crept through the dark-stained doors of Dundee Royal Infirmary. But Mrs Harkins set off like an arrow.

'This way,' she said, striding past the reception desk, and heading down a corridor. The boys followed her along the hall and into a large room. A woman dressed in white stood by a long desk, and a row of wooden chairs sat against the walls. A low, square table, dotted with wrinkled newspapers, stood at its centre.

'You boys get yerselves a seat. I'll away and see the nurse.' Mrs Harkins crossed to the woman in white.

After a brief, hushed chat, she came to sit beside the boys. 'Kevin's in room five,' she said. 'His mum and dad are in just now, but the Doctor's goin' tae see them in a minute. We'll just sit here and wait.'

No-one spoke a word, as they all sat and stared at the

black and white checked linoleum floor.

A few minutes later, the door opened. James looked up, expecting to see Kevin's parents. Instead, his eyes met with those of Teeny Robbins as she came through the doorway, followed by her mother. Teeny pulled at the sleeve of her mother's coat and whispered to her, while pointing at Aunt June. Mrs Robbins arched an eyebrow at James's aunt, and nodded towards Teeny.

Aunt June gave Teeny's mother a smile and nodded back. Teeny skipped towards the boys.

'Hello, James Gunning,' she said, sitting down beside him. 'My grandad's had tae come in with his gout. What're you lot here for?'

'It's Kevin. Something happened last night. A fire...' James's voice cracked as his throat tightened.

Teeny's face fell. 'Oh, no. Is he all right?'

'We don't know... We have to wait...'

The boys' heads snapped up as the ward door opened again and Kevin's family shuffled through it. His mother was sobbing inconsolably, as a nurse led them down the corridor.

James turned his red-rimmed eyes to his aunt.

'No, no' yet, James,' she said. 'Dinnae worry, the nurse'll tell us.'

They waited, the stillness broken only by the hollow ticking of a clock on the wall behind the desk. Teeny slid her hand under James's and curled her fingers round his.

This time, James was both aware and glad of it as they sat, hands clasped, and waited for the door to open.

⚮ ⚮ ⚮

'He can see you now,' the nurse said, kindly.

As the children stood up, Aunt June remained seated. 'He'll no' be needin' tae see me,' she said. 'He'll be wantin' tae see his pals.'

They inched towards the door. Teeny grasped James's hand even tighter. He squeezed back—somehow it made him feel a little braver. But when the nurse led them to another door, they hesitated for a moment, each one as anxious and afraid as the next.

Moving together, they crept inside, and gasped, as they saw what lay on the bed.

Every inch of Kevin's body was covered in bandages. The white strips were stained: dark red, brown, and sickly yellow. Kevin's head was also wrapped in dressings, all but his mouth, and one eye, which watched them as they drew nearer.

'Now, children, Kevin has asked to see you,' the nurse said. 'But his throat's very raw, and he can't talk too well. He's feeling awfully sore right now, so be sure you don't touch him.

'You can't stay for *too* long because we're about to move him to a special ward. So, I'll come and get you in a few minutes.' The nurse's voice was firm, but gentle.

'Excuse me,' James whispered.

'Yes?'

'Will... will Kevin be all right?'

The nurse's brow furrowed. Her eyes softened as she placed a hand on James's shoulder.

'We're doing the best we can for him,' she said, with a weak smile, which didn't hide the sadness in her eyes. She left the room, leaving the children alone.

For a moment, there was the deepest silence. No-one wanted to break it, but they knew they didn't have much time.

'Hey, Kevin,' Billy said, then seemed lost for words.

Ben opened his mouth to speak, but no words came.

James whispered. 'Oh, Kevin... it must have been *horrible.*'

A tear began to bead in the corner of Kevin's eye... and that was the very worst thing of all. That single tear engulfed them in sadness and they quietly wept. Each one ached to move to the bed and hold on to their friend, but knew they would only hurt him if they did.

'We'll get them, Kevin,' Derek said. Anger rose in his voice, as he brushed away his tears. 'We'll *do* McLintock for this. Him, and all of his stupid pals as well.'

The others nodded vigorously.

Kevin's mouth cracked open. The eye which the fire had spared, closed, and in a voice as dry as dust, he spoke in words they could barely hear.

'Not him. Paint...'

A dreadful silence fell.

'Oh no. The fire-pots...' James shuddered.

One of the paint pots had surely caught fire, or maybe fallen over onto the mass of blankets. Kevin had been trapped—alone—as the flames raged around him.

Ben turned and ran from the room. But James stepped to the edge of the bed. Teeny went with him, still clutching his hand.

With a touch as light as a feather, careful of the tubes and bandages, James laid his hand on Kevin's arm. Billy and Derek moved to Teeny's side and each placed a hand beside James's, making the same, slight, contact.

Kevin blinked his eye. He was still for a moment. Then, in that same, whisper-thin voice, he breathed, 'I'm... glad you came...'

Their tears began again, as the minutes ticked by in a sad stillness.

Then Billy spoke.

'We are all now blood brothers, forever and ever. We cannot be parted...' his voice faltered, as he tried to fight through the tears which closed up his throat.

Into that silence, Kevin whispered, '...for never... and... never.'

Then, for the last time, he fell asleep.

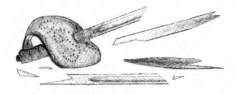

27

THE MAN IN BLACK

To the rest of the world, Monday was no different from any other day. Chimneys threw smoke into the pale September sky, Lochee's streets were filled with people hurrying on with their lives, and the steady pulse of the mills throbbed in the morning air.

But a hush hung over St Mary's morning assembly, as the Headmaster announced the news of Kevin's death. He ended the meeting by reminding the children of the dangers of playing with matches.

'He wasn't *playing* with them,' Billy hissed to James. 'He just knocked a pot over.'

James said nothing. Whether playing with matches or not, the fire had still been responsible for Kevin's accident.

The day dragged on. Billy, James, Ben and Derek drifted in and out during their lessons, only half-listening to their teacher. At the end of the day, they stepped out of the school gate and found themselves wrapped in smothering embraces by their waiting mothers. As the boys untangled themselves from the suffocating hugs, a voice came from behind them.

'Hey.'

They turned round, and their faces hardened.

'Beat it, McLintock!' Billy growled, fists clenched.

'William Harkins!' his mother gasped.

But, instead of the abuse they expected in return, John's eyes brimmed with tears. Confusion fell on the four boys, like a sudden shower of rain.

'What do you want?' James asked.

'I'm sorry,' mumbled McLintock. 'I didnae ken what had happened. I just heard today, when the teacher told us. We didnae really ken whaur yer den was. I'm really, really sorry.'

McLintock's words struck the boys like a blow.

He had lied.

And that lie had led to Kevin's accident. But, for him to come to them, apologetic and close to tears—it was too confusing. Not knowing what else to do, the boys stared at the ground.

Then Ben stepped out from the group. He extended his arm towards McLintock, who flinched, as if expecting some kind of punch. When none came, he stared at Ben's outstretched hand, then slowly reached out his own to shake it.

Following Ben's lead, James, Billy and Derek did likewise. Once the handshakes were done an awkward silence settled onto the boys.

McLintock coughed. 'Well, I huvtae get home,' he said, and walked off up the hill, occasionally glancing back over his shoulder.

'Aw, that was nice, eh? Is that you lads pals now?' Billy's mother asked.

'He's not our pal,' said Billy. 'But maybe he won't be as annoying as he has been.'

'Maybe,' Derek said, as John turned around the corner of the High Street.

As they walked home, the boys' mothers spoke about the war, sharing their worries about rationing as the conflict dragged on. But the boys were lost in their own deep discussion—debating whether or not McLintock had truly turned over a new leaf—or if he would start to annoy them again after some time had passed.

Suddenly, the adults stopped mid-stride.

'Oh no. Oh, James,' Mrs Harkins said, her hand covering her mouth.

It jolted the boys from their buzzing chatter. James peered into the distance, puzzled, wondering what had shocked Aunt June so. And then he saw it, sitting outside the tenement close—an olive-green motorcycle.

James's stomach lurched as a chill ran through him.

He snatched his hand from his aunt's and ran. He flew straight for the tenement, almost charging *through* people—uncaring if there were carts, or trams, or motorcars on the road between him and the close.

'Daaadyyyyy! Noooooo!' he screamed.

His friends ran after him; their mothers bellowed at them to slow down, to be careful, to come back—but they were beyond hearing.

James entered the close at full speed and took the stairs two at a time, his heart hammering in his chest. He reached for the doorknob, but couldn't turn it.

Stop worrying. He's probably not even at this house. He fought with himself to be brave, dreading what he might find inside.

Then another, stranger, idea came into his head.

If there is a God of All Small Boys, the Telegram Man won't be here.

A cold, hollow thought immediately followed. *But Kevin still died.*

The others thundered out of the stairwell.

'James…' they all said at once.

'I can't open the door,' James whispered. 'I can't…'

Billy took James's hand from the doorknob, and Derek reached out and turned it.

The door swung open.

The house seemed darker than normal. From inside, the boys could only just hear the faint rumble of a male voice.

THE GOD OF ALL SMALL BOYS

James's face crumpled, as his tears spilled over. 'Oh, Billy,' he whispered. 'I'm scared. I can't move my feet.'

Billy placed his hand on James shoulder. 'Just take one step at a time. We're right behind you.'

James shuffled into the house, as though he were walking through treacle. The living room seemed miles away, as he inched toward the closed, forbidding door. He could hear his uncle's voice, but his heart hammered so loudly he could barely make anything out.

Then the words "*shot*", and, "*we'd heard a lot of people from here had been killed*", filtered through the door, and James's alarm overcame his fear. He sprang into the room.

'NO! NOT MY DADDY!' he screamed—then he froze.

For as long as he lived, James would remember that moment of utter terror.

Fresh tears spilled, blurring the vision of his uncle, who stood beside the fire. A tall man stood in front of him, his back to the door, wearing the unmistakeable uniform of *The Telegram Man*. His boots, trousers and jacket were almost jet black, the long coat made of battered, dark leather. In his left hand he held the only item which was not black: the white-banded cap of the feared motorcycle man.

Wait! A thought forced its way through James's panic. *That isn't a cap. It looks like a bandage...*

192

And then the man turned around.

It took James a full three seconds to realise he was gazing into the face of his father. Then, without another sound, he ran to be enclosed in an embrace he had been wishing for, since that bright and dreadful autumn day, forever ago.

✝ ✝ ✝

Mr Gunning had been lucky—extremely lucky.

While leading an assault on the German lines—his sword held high, and his revolver in his hand—a bullet had punched into his left arm. The slug smashed the bone, breaking it in two places, then ricocheted out and struck his sword. The blade shattered, throwing large slivers of sharp metal into his right arm.

The doctors had left the captain in no doubt—his broken arm would heal, but the injuries to the muscles in his right arm were permanent. He would never again be able to raise it above chest height.

He could not lift a rifle to his eye. He could not use a gun.

His war was over.

28

THE GOD OF ALL SMALL BOYS

James and his father had stayed the night with the Harkins', and the next morning they were picked up by Mr Gunning's driver, to be taken back to Cedar Road. The Harkins and the Wilsons barely had time to say goodbye, as James ran to the car.

He knelt on the seat and waved through the back window, until the figures were lost around the bend of the High Street. The car left Lochee and drove through Dundee to the riverside. Sunlight caught the water, making it sparkle. The trees which lined its banks hung with red and gold leaves, as the season hurried on. Soon, they reached Cedar Road and crunched up the gravelled driveway.

As James jumped from the car, the unmistakeable tang of the Tay reached him. He smiled, having almost forgotten that green, salty smell. Then he ran to the house, where Mary and Toosh met him with open arms, and smiles as wide as the river. He could barely breathe in their crushing embrace, but he didn't mind the tiniest bit.

Every door in the house was open, every window flung wide, to air the house after the long weeks of lying empty. It was a day of tears and smiles and many moments when James thought he would burst with joy.

But that night, as he lay in his own bed, there seemed to be too much space. It felt strange, to be able to stretch out and not hit Billy in the face, and to not have the twins' feet jammed under his nose.

In the half-light, he stared at his ceiling, and a sudden, sad thought hit him.

I didn't get to say goodbye to Christina. I wonder if she misses me, or even cares that I'm gone.

But behind all of his wonderings, despite the fresh sheets and comfortable bed, one larger thought overtook them all—and it was that which settled in his mind, as he finally drifted to sleep.

I'm home.

✝ ✝ ✝

In the days that followed, it became very clear to James that the war had changed his father. His injuries had ended his days of fighting, so he had been placed in charge of the Army Recruitment Office in Dundee. He played with James more often, and far easier than he had before, and seemed more willing to talk and laugh with James—even about things which were unimportant and silly.

But, the absolute best thing of all was that his father hugged him so much more, and for no other reason than that they were together.

Four days after his return home, James arrived back in Lochee, to attend the funeral service for Kevin. As he and his father came within view of St Mary's Church James broke into a run, to be met by Derek, Ben and Billy.

'You found your way back then?' Derek grinned.

'James. Look. My dad's got his Service Badge! Did you know your dad got him a job with the Black Watch?' Billy asked.

James nodded, but before he could reply someone grabbed him from behind.

'Look at you, James Gunning! Comin' back here in yer posh clothes, tryin' tae show us up!'

'Christina...' James turned, his voice hoarse with emotion.

Before he could say another word she flung her arms around his neck, squeezed him tight, and planted a kiss on his cheek. The boys stared, faces frozen with shock. James's face burned red, but he smiled, as Teeny took him by the hand and led him into the Chapel.

They joined the congregation and—because no-one would have been able to stop her—Teeny Robbins sat with James throughout the service. They held hands and wept quietly together, as their friend was laid to rest.

⧎ ⧎ ⧎

The last days of autumn passed. The chestnuts dropped from the trees, and winter crept into Dundee. James returned to Lochee whenever he could. His blood-brother bond with Ben, Derek and Billy deepened—and his friendship with Teeny blossomed—as his father occasionally shuttled his friends to Broughty Ferry, for visits which never seemed to last long enough.

Then, one day in late November, Mr Gunning asked his son if he would like his friends to sleep over during the winter holidays—and to visit for Christmas, and Easter, and any other time he wanted. That same invitation was also extended to the Harkins, or as his father now called them, *his family*.

It was as if the wish James had made back in the den had been granted, and he could hardly say '*YES!*' for hugging his father so tight.

A few days before Christmas, Billy, Derek, Teeny and Ben spent a glorious day at Cedar Road. After they had been taken home, as night began to fall, James stared out of his bedroom window. He knelt up on his bed, looking out into the approaching night, watching the pale, winter sun dip towards the Tay. He remembered the times when he and his friends had watched that same sun—falling towards the same river—from their viewpoint at the den.

A gentle tap at the door interrupted James's thoughts, as his father came into the room and sat on the bed.

'How are you, son?' he asked. 'You've been very quiet tonight. I thought seeing your friends today would have cheered you up? They really liked the Christmas tree, didn't they—especially Christina. Should I be planning a wedding anytime soon?'

James blushed, deeply. 'Daa-aad!' he said, reflecting his father's smile, but not meeting his eyes.

'Seriously, though. Is anything wrong, James?'

Tears filled James's eyes. He threw his arms around his father's neck and began to weep. Captain Gunning held his son tight and waited for him to speak.

'I keep thinking about Kevin,' James eventually said, snuffling. 'He stayed in Lochee all his life, in all that smoke and noise. He never got a chance to see all of this. He never saw the sun coming up out of the sea—I don't even think he ever visited a beach. He'll never be able to hold hands with a pretty girl, or go to *big school*, or even get a job.

'How can he be *dead*, Daddy? I don't understand! It

isn't *fair!*' James's sobs began again and his father held him closer.

'It's not an easy thing, son,' he said, his voice quiet and steady. 'I saw many young men fall in France... *too* many. And for each one, I felt terribly sad, knowing they would never grow into the men they could have become. They left behind wives, girlfriends, children—even parents. And every one of them will be mourned by their families and friends forever.

'But James, none of them would *ever* have wanted their loved-ones to live the rest of their lives in sadness. If I had died...' he stopped, as James whimpered against his shoulder, and clung to him even tighter.

The captain stroked James's hair, then eased back and cradled his son's face in his hands. 'If I had died,' he repeated. 'I would not have wanted *you* to live your life in sorrow. Oh, it is right and proper that we should mourn the dead, and *of course* we feel sad when they pass. But we must remember—they have gone on to a better life than this one.'

He kissed James's forehead, then stood up, leaned on the windowsill and stared outside.

'It's much like what happened with your mother.'

James almost stopped breathing. His father had never really spoken of his mother. Not to him—not like this.

Mr Gunning bowed his head, his eyes glistened in the half-light. James longed to dash to his father, but, before he could do so, the captain moved to kneel by the bedside.

'I met her quite by chance, James. I was your age, and she was about the same age as your little Christina. It was simple luck that allowed us to spend most of our time together. We married on my twenty-first birthday, and on the day you were born I thought I would never stop smiling. For five years we were the happiest family on earth.

'Then, when she died, I thought I would never smile again. But I *knew*, in the deepest part of my heart, that she would have been *horrified* if I had gone on to live in darkness and melancholy for the rest of my life. But we *are* only human, son, and we cannot *help* being sad.

'So, we cry, and we miss those people terribly. But the time will always come when we cannot cry anymore. And when that happens, there is one very important thing which we all must learn. Just one thing. Shall I tell you what it is?'

James nodded.

'We need to learn to let go, son.' His father took a long breath and gave a deep sigh. 'Oh, James, it is so very difficult, I do not deny it. But as you grow older you will realise that it is possible to love someone—even beyond death—and still be able to let them go.

'We cannot live every moment regretting what they did not do. Instead, we should feel glad for the time we had with them. After a while, you will find that you can think of them without bringing yourself more grief. So, we must let ourselves *smile* at their memory—and allow them to bring us joy again.

'Do you understand, James? Do you think you can do that?'

James's face still glittered with tears. He bit at his bottom lip and tried to smile as he nodded.

'That's my brave boy. Goodnight, son. Sleep well. I'll see you in the morning.' The captain kissed James on the forehead and left the room.

James's mind whirled, bursting with a million thoughts of his parents and his friends. He knelt up on his bed again and stared back out of the window, to find the sky had turned a deep, dark blue.

'*On the ba', Dundee.*' He whispered, while streaks of scarlet and purple tore across the low clouds, as night unfolded over the city.

He watched the sky changing its colours, as it had on that perfect day at the den—when heaven had been a hole in the ground. He thought of Kevin, and of all the things he and his friends had done during those few, long—but all-too-short—days.

And as he watched—as the sunlight faded, and the stars came into their own—James spoke to Kevin one last time.

He whispered his secrets: about his feelings of love

for his father, his family and friends—and for Christina. He said his goodbyes, told Kevin that he would always remember him and then he let him go:

To a place where the summer went on and on, and every night the sun set as if the sky was ablaze. Where *The God of All Small Boys* smiled kindly upon his charges— ever watchful—as they ran, faster than any child could run, and laughed and played along streets where no carts, or trams, or cars would ever rumble past.

To a place where lightning storms could rage and thunder—but cause no fear, only a wild and shrieking joy. Where trees waited to be discovered, with branches aching to be climbed. Where every boy or girl could find all of the answers, to all the secrets that had ever been.

To a place where they could wallow in the long, cool, yellow grass— smelling of wet puppies and spent fireworks—that swayed like a restless sea and, somehow, seemed to stretch out and away… into forever.

THE END

ACKNOWLEDGEMENTS

MASSIVE thanks to Anne Glennie for her belief, trust, and time—moulding this into a finished product—and to Charlotte for her amazing illustrations.

As well as thanking you for reading this, I should mention...
My parents Joe and Mary. My siblings Christine (Toosh) and Derek. The myriad of family: Gunnings and Hays and Moirs and Flights. The Livvy Squad: Rab, Steve, John, Ritchie. Tracey and the Harkins, and The Martins.

Norman Gudmunsen for encouraging a small boy's scrawlings in the mid-70s.
Fellow scribbler, Harvey Duke, for surviving Halley's Mill in the mid-80s.
Special thanks to my dear friends Jock Ferguson and John McLintock.
Mrs Conroy and Mr Marra (St. Mary's Primary)
Theresa Jones (#pitchwarriors) for a second pair of eyes on the first draft.

And finally, to #ClanCranachan—my extended literary family—hoping we all go on to greater heights! Much love to you all!

ABOUT THE AUTHOR

Before turning to children's fiction, Joseph Lamb wrote historical dramas which were performed throughout Scotland. Much of his creative output is set in Scotland, with a focus on his home town of Dundee—where he lives with his wife and two children.

An actor with over 30 years' experience, Joseph frequently undertakes school visits and public events, based around his historical writing work—covering eras from the Vikings, to the Jacobites, and beyond.

@joecovenant
www.joecovenant.com
www.facebook.com/TheGodOfAllSmallBoys/

YOU MIGHT ALSO ENJOY...

The Beast on the Broch
by John K. Fulton
Scotland, 799 AD. Talorca befriends a strange Pictish
beast; together, they fight off Viking raiders.

Charlie's Promise
by Annemarie Allan
A frightened refugee arrives in Scotland on the
brink of WW2 and needs Charlie's help.

Fir for Luck
by Barbara Henderson
The heart-wrenching tale of a girl's courage to save her
village from the Highland Clearances.

A Pattern of Secrets
by Lindsay Littleson
Jim must save his brother from the Poor House in
this gripping Victorian mystery.

Punch
by Barbara Henderson
Runaway Phin's journey across Victorian Scotland with
an escaped prisoner and a dancing bear.

The Revenge of Tirpitz
by M. L. Sloan
The thrilling WW2 story of a boy's role in the sinking
of the warship Tirpitz.